# THE BEST FRIEND INCIDENT

a Driven to Love romantic comedy

*Enjoy!
Smooches!
Melia Alexander
09.09.19*

# THE BEST FRIEND INCIDENT

a Driven to Love romantic comedy

# MELIA ALEXANDER

This book is a work of fiction. Names, characters, places, and incidents are the product of the author's imagination or are used fictitiously. Any resemblance to actual events, locales, or persons, living or dead, is coincidental.

Copyright © 2018 by Melia Alexander. All rights reserved, including the right to reproduce, distribute, or transmit in any form or by any means. For information regarding subsidiary rights, please contact the Publisher.

Entangled Publishing, LLC
2614 South Timberline Road
Suite 105, PMB 159
Fort Collins, CO 80525
Visit our website at www.entangledpublishing.com.

Lovestruck is an imprint of Entangled Publishing, LLC.

Edited by Heather Howland
Cover design by Heather Howland
Cover art from iStock

Manufactured in the United States of America

First Edition April 2018

*To Kevin. Thank you for bourbon tastings…Beauty and the Beast…chasing waterfalls…Napa…midnight laughter…and morning smiles! Mostly, thank you for inspiring me to be the best version of myself possible. I am forever grateful.*

# Chapter One

Stacey Winters stopped outside her apartment door, steeling herself with a breath of cool, central Oregon air. This was it. Her boyfriend was back in Milestone, and tonight, they were taking their five-week relationship to the next level. Leo had texted that he'd picked up the key she'd left at the music venue where he'd perform this week, and would be on the other side of her door, waiting.

For her.

Stacey shivered. With anticipation, of course. This guy was "the one," she was sure of it.

It didn't make her any less nervous, though.

*Focus.* She slid her key into the lock. Seriously. How come the first time with a guy was always so nerve-racking? Leo was rock-star hot—fitting, since music was, in fact, what he did for a living. Really, she needed to just relax and enjoy the ride.

She paused in the doorway. Wait. Was that an Ariana Grande ballad drifting down the hallway from her bedroom? She blinked, and fluttering butterflies took flight in her belly.

He'd put on something she enjoyed instead of playing his own music on a constant loop? That was…unexpected. And very, very sweet.

Softly closing the door behind her, Stacey surveyed the dim room…and spotted a trail of rose petals leading down the carpeted hallway. She pressed a hand to her chest, like she could actually touch the melty giddiness coursing through her. That was exactly the kind of romance she loved, and here he was, serving it up on a rose petal–covered platter.

Further proof that she and Leo were meant to be together, right?

She grinned. The rest of her life was clicking into place — all that was missing was her lifelong, hopelessly romantic dream of being part of a head-over-heels-in-love couple. After a string of failures, it was about time she found her *real* match.

Anticipation gripped her heart as she followed the trail of fragile petals. Tomorrow she'd gather them and preserve them in a keepsake box. It'd be fun to have something to show her and Leo's grandchildren. But right now, it was time for the best kind of adult fun.

Her bedroom was like the deep end of a cave, thanks to the blackout curtains she'd installed, but soft snores filled the space. From the sound of things, Leo was jet-lagged. Three weeks touring with his band in Asia was bound to catch up with him. At least he was here.

She bit her lip. Should she wake him up or let him sleep? He'd been just as eager to do this when they'd last spoken…

*Seize the moment.* The phrase might be clichéd, but Stacey had sworn by it since she was a child. In a world that only rewarded action, you had to create what you wanted. Case in point, she was in the middle of turning her passion project, Dinners for Two, into a thriving company.

*Waking him up it is.* If he wasn't interested, she'd settle for a night of snuggling.

She pulled off her boots and socks, then moved on to her jeans. Leo would have plenty of opportunities to take her clothes off tomorrow. It was a shame he wouldn't see her new coordinated panty and bra set, though. The lace brushed against her nipples when she pulled her sweater off to join the pile of clothing on the floor, and she shivered. She'd felt bold, brazen, and totally in control the second she'd slipped on the pieces earlier that afternoon, and she clung to that confidence as she stood in her pitch-black room, trying to decide the best way to tempt a sleeping man back into consciousness.

Hands out, she shuffled forward, groping for her bed. It wasn't quite the same thing as strutting across the room in a thong and high heels, but that was okay. She'd rock his world once she got into bed. If she could find the dang thing.

Her hands found their target and she crawled in. But instead of warm male skin, she encountered denim. Stacey frowned. Leo was still fully dressed and lying on his side, facing the framed print of Chinaman Hat that hung on her wall.

That he was facing that particular print made the situation even more exciting. At her sister's urging, Stacey had followed local folklore and burned an offering at that very mountain a couple of months ago, all in order to find her true love.

Shortly after that, she'd met Leo when he and his band played at the resort near Chinaman Hat at the exact time she'd set a Dinners for Two event. It seemed fitting to have found the love of her life on the same night she'd helped another couple with their own happily ever after.

How was *that* for fate?

She leaned toward him, breathed in deeply, and frowned. The allergy meds she'd taken earlier must be messing with her because he smelled…different. Familiar, but not what she expected. Maybe she'd forgotten what he smelled like. It *had* been a few weeks, and they hadn't spent that much time together before he left.

Never mind that, though. Concentrating, she reached out a hand and trailed her fingers over his upper arm.

Leo didn't move.

Hmm. She traced her fingers back toward his shoulder. *Nice muscles.* Better than she remembered. He'd been talking about hitting the gym when the tour ended, laughing that he'd need to bulk up if he were to keep up with her need for adventure, but clearly he'd gotten a head start. He must've wanted it to be a surprise, and she *definitely* wasn't complaining.

She'd joked with her best friend, Grant, that she could only get serious about a guy who was fit enough to mountain bike around the trails at Chinaman Hat. There wasn't a doubt now that he'd make it.

Slowly, deliberately, she rubbed her breasts against his bare arm, loving the friction so much her nipples tightened into hard peaks underneath the thin lace.

She brushed a kiss across his cheek, felt the stubble on her lips, and smiled. Stacey closed her eyes and, to the beat of Ariana Grande's sexy, sensual song, slowly trailed a line of kisses toward his mouth. He turned, capturing her lips and parting for her.

She whimpered. His lips were full, soft, the sense of familiarity and homecoming so palpable her heart ached. So good...

The kiss started off gentle, sweet. His tongue swept into her mouth, teased hers until she moaned. Delicious tingles raced through her as the kiss deepened, intensifying until every nerve ending pulsed with an awareness Stacey had never experienced before.

She shifted, straddling him as he ran his hands over her hips, her waist... She'd known she'd wanted Leo, but until now she hadn't realized how *badly* she wanted him. Anticipation pooled between her legs, his kisses searing her, touching a part of her soul. And that's when she knew deep down that she'd truly, *finally* found "the one."

It was about damned time.

· · ·

*Somethin' 'bout you makes me feel like a dangerous woman...*

Grant Phillips wasn't a big believer in dreams or what they meant, but he did believe in living in the moment, and so far, Ariana Grande was *un-fucking-believable*. If he made her feel like a dangerous woman, that was fine by him. The passion in her words translated to the hot kisses she trailed across his cheek, to the way she captured his mouth, and definitely to the way she pressed her tits against him.

*Somethin' 'bout you makes me wanna do things that I shouldn't...*

And why not? They were both adults...

Grant turned, wrapped an arm around her small waist, and let his hand trail up one side as she straddled him.

*Oh yeah, baby.*

He lifted his hips and deepened the kiss until she moaned and ground herself against him. A moment later, her citrus scent registered. She smelled like freshly picked lemons. He liked lemons. A lot.

Lemons?

Wait. There was only one woman he knew who smelled like lemons...

He stilled his hands, forced his fuzzy, sleep-deprived brain into gear, and shifted just enough so he could reach for the bedside lamp. In the sudden circle of light, he blinked, felt the weight of the woman on him, and heard her gasp all at the same time as two things registered.

First, Ariana Grande wasn't there. Second, he hadn't seen his best friend so pissed off since the time he hid a harmless garter snake in her locker back in high school. Only now, it didn't make much sense. What was she—

"Grant! What the hell?"

He stared at the startled expression on Stacey's face, then glanced around the room. He was in her bed. She was straddling his lap, naked. Kinda naked, anyway. The barely-there black lace she wore didn't technically count as clothing, did it?

Then the whole evening came rushing back at him in stunning clarity. That night's awful first date…the need to hash through the gory details with his best friend while they watched Netflix… Only, when he'd arrived at her apartment, Stacey's jerk boyfriend was already there.

By the time he'd gotten rid of the guy, Grant was too tired to pull out the laptop and load an action flick. He'd put some music on and crashed on her bed instead. Just like he'd done countless times.

"What the *fucking hell* are you doing here?" she demanded again.

*Oh, shit.* He really wasn't dreaming.

"Stacey." His voice was hoarse. From shock, no doubt. After all, how often did a guy see his best friend almost as naked as the day she came into this world?

She crossed her arms over her breasts and scrambled off him, but not before he got an eyeful of her gorgeously ripe nipples pushing against the black lace, or saw the mortification stamped on her face.

The hell of it was, his dick hadn't gotten word that the woman he'd been playing a tongue duet with had turned out to be the one woman whose friendship he'd never risk losing. His hands, either, because they tried to grab her back. He fisted the sheets and hoped she didn't cut them off.

The look she shot him was hard. Carbon steel hard, and he was pretty sure if they were back on their old grade-school playground, she'd deck him. Hell, he wasn't convinced that right now, crouched on the floor and peeking up at him, she wouldn't attempt something like that again. "Where's Leo?"

Leo? Oh, right. Her latest in a long line of guys she'd sworn was "the one." "I threw him out."

"Why the hell did you do that?" The words were quietly spoken, but she was pissed. All that anger would erupt into a firestorm in about three...two...

"You had no right to throw him out!" Her voice inched up an octave, which, given how long they'd known each other, wasn't much of a surprise. Indignation and rage rose out of her eyes like steam from the copper still at Mile High Desert Distillery where he worked.

Her eyes continued doing the fire and brimstone thing. "Just who the hell do you think you are, Grant Phillips? The King of Milestone? I want you out of my apartment. Now."

He frowned. Did she really not know her boyfriend was a cheating bastard? Did he want to be the one to tell her the guy'd had his wedding ring on and was talking to another woman when Grant had let himself in?

He began to sit up. "Stace—"

"Don't you *dare* move." She glared at him, her brown eyes on the verge of becoming lethal weapons.

"Leave. Don't move. Make up your mind, already." He leaned back again and looked pointedly at her. "Why don't you put a robe on or something?"

"Turn on your side."

No problem there. He rolled away, only to catch her reflection in the glass covering the framed print of Chinaman Hat on the wall. He tried to pull his gaze away, but damn it, his brain seemed to have decided he liked what he was seeing.

She had curves. Gorgeous curves. On someone so

petite she could've appeared plump, but she wasn't. She was perfectly proportioned. Her long, brown hair, normally in a ponytail, flowed freely down her back. Tugging on it could be a lot of fun…

What the hell was he doing? He shouldn't be thinking about things like that, and he shouldn't be staring, either. After all, Stacey was like a *sister* to him. They'd grown up together, and she was the first friend he'd made when he'd been sent to live with his foster parents. His *first* set of foster parents.

She was his best friend, damn it.

He pulled his gaze away from the glass when she yanked her closet door open. "You've got some nerve, you know that?"

He swallowed, then took a stab at the conversation, hoping she hadn't caught him staring like a prepubescent boy. "For what? Throwing Cleo out? I was doing you a favor."

"Leo," she said. "His name is Leo."

"Leo the liar," he muttered. If there was one thing Grant couldn't stand, it was liars. Like the foster parents who'd sworn over and over there was nothing wrong with him, even as they turned him over to his next set of temporary parents.

"What?"

Damn it. He hated to be the one to tell her. Really, it was disappointing. Hadn't he taught her enough about his species to make an intelligent choice in the guy department? "What the hell were you thinking, giving a complete stranger a key to your place?"

"We've been dating for five weeks, moron."

"Yeah, and he's been gone for three of those five weeks." He'd heard enough of her pining after the idiot to know that much. "Do the math. He's practically a stranger. Plus, he had that stupid trail of rose petals to your bedroom."

"It's *romantic*. Not that you'd understand."

Romantic? He rolled his eyes. "Guys only do stuff like that so they can get laid."

"Maybe I wanted to get laid."

He grimaced, but not for the right reasons. He did *not* like the idea of that asshat touching her. "Should we be having this conversation? You know, since I'm in your bed and all?"

"Very funny. You can turn around now."

He turned over, then scooted to a sitting position on the bed, just like all the other times he'd been in it while they watched Netflix and ate popcorn. One thing was for sure, he'd probably never be able to watch another movie in bed with her without remembering the feel of her body on his.

"Look, Stace, if he really cared about you, he'd have made a trail to the kitchen where there'd be dinner. But instead, what'd he do? He had his dick ready and waiting in your bed." Sort of, anyway. When Grant had walked in, the guy was pacing her living room, telling some "babe" that he was in Cleveland. He'd even had the nerve to hold his finger up in the universal signal for Grant to remain quiet. And that's when he'd seen the wedding band. Bastard.

Shit. If he was gonna tell her, there wasn't ever really a good time, was there? Might as well get it over with. "He's married."

"What?" Her eyes widened. "He is *not* married." She slowly enunciated every word and crossed her arms, then her eyes narrowed into thin slits. "How could you say that?"

"Because it's true." He shoved a hand through his hair. "Look, do you think I'd tell you something like that if it *wasn't* true? Think about it. The guy's never in Milestone except for a few days here. Just enough time to play a couple of concerts, then he's off to the next stop. Or so he says. What do you really know about him, Stace?"

She stuck her chin out, a mixture of defiance and flat-out adorableness.

He gave himself a mental shake. Adorable wasn't how he should be referring to his best friend.

"If that's true," she said, "how come he's never pressed me to sleep with him?"

"Do I really have to answer that?" Grant knew his species, knew that guys like Leo would prey on any female who seemed remotely willing. And if one said no it didn't matter, because there was always one who would say yes.

He took a deep breath. "I saw his wedding ring."

"Oh, God." The whispered words tugged at his heart, made him clench his fists. He should've punched the asshole before throwing him out.

Her shoulders sagged and her face crumpled for a moment, just long enough for him to recognize the pain and disappointment. But there'd be no tears. As sensitive as Stacey was, he hadn't seen her cry since they were in grade school. And back then it was because she'd given a boy a black eye for pulling on her braids.

She swallowed, lifted her chin, and her face morphed back into a woman in control. "I guess he wasn't the guy I thought he was after all."

"Hey, I'm sorry."

"That's it. I'm done with this conversation." She stared at him, her eyes flashing as she crossed her arms. "Get out. Now."

Not until he'd done damage control. He folded his hands behind his head and settled in. "Shouldn't we talk about this? You know, they say couples should never go to bed angry."

"I've seriously had it, Grant."

"Fine." So much for trying to lighten the mood. Under normal circumstances she'd have taken his lead and they'd be laughing by now. He blew out a breath and rolled off the bed, then reached for his sneakers. "For the record, you were the one kissing me."

"Because I thought you were someone else."

Ouch.

Okay, he'd asked for that. But why should he be surprised? Through all the years they'd known each other, not once had there been anything like that kiss between them. The thought had crossed his mind, but he didn't do the kind of relationship Stacey was after.

Relationships weren't permanent. Neither was love. Not for someone like him, anyway. Grant reached for the other shoe. Still, it was too bad. He kinda liked the kiss.

Wait. That was a stupid thought, one destined to have him severing his friendship with the only woman he'd allowed close enough to know him, warts and all. She was his best friend, for God's sake. That's where the relationship belonged. Firmly in the friend zone.

And that's where they'd stay.

# Chapter Two

Stacey snuggled deeper under the covers, languishing in the space between dream and reality, and fighting desperately to keep her eyelids shut. It seemed like no matter how late she fell asleep, her body was damned determined to rouse her out of bed at almost exactly seven a.m. So much for the blackout curtains.

She'd spent part of the evening waiting for Leo to call, finally texting him around midnight. After a heated text-battle-turned-phone-call, she discovered he really *was* married.

Asshole.

Then she'd spent the better part of last night trying to forget what it felt like to straddle Grant, to touch him, to be touched by him. Even now her body responded, tightening at the memory of him, the feel of him, his kisses…

She rolled onto one side. Really, it was a simple mistake, right? Best to forget about it, and definitely no need to make a big deal out of it. She'd put their friendship back on firmer footing, back in a place that made sense.

Her brain understood the concept. Her body, on the other hand… She clenched her thighs together and tamped down the rush of longing. She'd never reacted that way with any of the guys she'd dated. Ever. But she wasn't silly enough to believe that Grant was anywhere in the running for anything other than being her best friend, and he had that position pretty well tied down.

Even if he was a viable option, he didn't want a relationship. The fact that they were good friends, the best of friends, was more than enough for Stacey. It had to be.

No denying he'd been as aroused as she'd been, but he was a guy. In that situation any guy would've reacted the same way. Bottom line: Grant still wasn't relationship material. End of discussion.

There. It was so much better when her brain was functioning logically. Besides, it wasn't unusual for him to be in her bed. They'd been sitting with their backs on the headboard, watching movies off her laptop for years.

Today was a new day. She'd get up—eventually—and head to her favorite coffee shop. It'd get her out of her apartment, something she needed to do if she was going to encourage the universe to send her "the one." Maybe she'd go back to online dating... Nah, none of those dates had ever worked out. How could a computer algorithm possibly compete with what the universe had in store for her? She needed to meet him organically, and she would.

Still, last night's memories lingered in her head, a reel of chick flicks and action movies that had her somewhere between awareness and oblivion, just on the precipice of falling asleep again.

*Clank.*

*What the hell?* Her eyes flew open, and she sat up and gripped the sheets, her gaze zeroing in on her half-closed bedroom door. Her heart hammered. Was that a real sound or one of those annoying dream-state intrusions designed to get a person's ass out of bed?

It had to be the dream thing. No one would be in her apartment. No one. Despite the assurances, her heart thumped out a fast beat, and fear clutched at her chest. Which was totally silly. She was safe. She'd chosen her apartment in one of the safest, lower rent areas of the city. Her dad had approved, and so had Grant.

And Grant was only a few blocks over, close enough that it'd take him less than two minutes to get here if she needed him. But she didn't need him because *no one was here*. She was alone and her brain was playing funky tricks on her. Really, she needed to get it under control.

Wait. Was that a crinkling sound? She strained to listen. Where the hell was it coming from? Her heartbeat kicked up again, and a shot of adrenaline hit her system.

*Breathe.*

Her phone? Where was her phone? Shit. She'd deliberately left it in the kitchen to charge after her oh-so-unpleasant conversation with Leo last night. In the end, she'd had to block his number.

Her heart pounded as she considered her options. She was on the third story, so climbing out the window wasn't a good idea. Unless she could tie some bedsheets together?

*Get a grip, Stacey.* What had her father always taught her? That it was easier to come up with a solution when you had control over your emotions. Not that he'd ever been hunted by a serial killer in broad daylight before. At least, she didn't think that'd ever happened to him.

There was that crinkling sound again. Maybe the killer was getting duct tape out so he could tie her up, keep her quiet. Then God knew what the hell else he'd do. The hairs on the back of her neck bristled. Damn Grant and his insistence on watching action thrillers when it was his turn to pick a movie.

Okay, that did it. She wasn't going to be a victim. Not

ever, and definitely not in her own home. She pulled the bedcovers aside and fumbled for the closest hard object on her nightstand. So far, there were no other sounds coming from the apartment's main room, but just in case the killer was still there, she couldn't march out with only words as a weapon. She'd never cursed her 5'2" height before, but damn she wished she were taller. Broader. Meaner.

Well, she could certainly act mean. She crept toward the door and peered outside. Whoever was there wasn't going to know what hit him.

. . .

Grant swore under his breath. Changing out a lock was supposed to be a piece of cake, but it was ten times harder when a guy had to be quiet while he did it.

There was no other way to get it done, though, since there was a better than fair chance that Stacey would never agree. It was his fault for forgetting to get the key back from her creepazoid boyfriend, so it was either this or Grant would have to stand post. God knew he didn't have time to take that on.

The screwdriver slipped out of his fingers and dropped onto the tile entryway. It was so damned quiet the *clank* reverberated down the hallway as well as past the one earbud he had in, and the blast of Linkin Park coming through it.

Shit.

He glanced behind him at the rose petal path that still led the way to Stacey's bedroom. He'd deliberately left one earbud out so he could hear her coming, but hoped to hell he could get this done and be out of here before she woke up. As pissed as she was last night, he was pretty sure this wasn't going to make anything better, but he had a responsibility to keep her safe. That's what best friends did for each other.

Which is why he had to forget the sensual feel of her

moving against him…the way his own hands had stolen over her naked back, held her hips in place…

Damn it. He sucked in a deep breath. If he wasn't careful, he'd throw away the most important relationship he'd ever had all because of a kiss. Yeah, Stacey was *that* important to him. She was fun and interesting and understanding and—

"Grant Adam Phillips. What the *hell* do you think you're doing?"

—and at the moment she was thoroughly pissed at him. Again.

"Making tea," he said. With the partially opened door between his knees, he twisted the existing knob, slid each side off, then set the parts off to one side.

"Don't get smart with me."

"You know you sound like your mom when you say that."

He stood…and nearly fell over. He should've prepared himself before facing her. Her hair was mussed and she wore a tiny pair of shorts with a thin, see-through top that stopped just above of her waist. She was rumpled and sexy and standing in front of him like the sweetest of temptations.

"Very funny, wiseass. Answer the question already."

The question? He scoured his brain for an answer. He should say something, preferably something intelligent that'd break through this weirdness between them, this strange pull that demanded he take a step toward her, demanded he haul her over his shoulder and back to her bedroom. Then they could finish what they'd started last night.

Always the mind reader, her lips parted, and her gaze met his. Confusion, uncertainty, lust. All three melded together in her whiskey-colored eyes. It wouldn't take much. Two steps, maybe.

Then she shifted, and his gaze flickered downward. Whoa. Was that…

He gulped. "Stace, what are you holding?"

# Chapter Three

Stacey blinked and followed Grant's gaze. Oh, shit. Her dildo. She was hanging onto her dildo like a club. Of all the hard objects she possessed within grabbing distance, she'd grabbed *her dildo* off her nightstand.

Her whole body flushed and she yanked her hand behind her back. "Nothing." She shook her head, willing it to be so. "It's nothing."

His gaze narrowed. "Then why are you turning red?"

"Don't try to change the subject." She cleared her throat, hoping to heaven some of the mortification would go along with it. "I'm really mad at you. How'd you get in here?"

"I've had a key for, like, five years, remember?"

Oh, shit. That's right. She gave herself a mental shake. "I mean, why the hell are you changing the lock?"

That's it. Keep the topic focused on him and away from the fact she'd had to use her toy just to get to sleep last night.

But he wasn't having any of it. "Did I interrupt something? You want me to leave?"

She heard the words, but she also heard the lust behind

them, saw the way he'd stepped toward her, felt the heat from his body, and saw the deeper question in his eyes.

She shook her head. "No."

"You want me to stay?"

Shit. How did she answer *that*? "Yes. No." Both sounded like great options, and for the same reason. She shook her head, felt another spike of heat to her face. Too bad she couldn't melt into the floor.

Grant slowly dragged his gaze down her body and back up again, the movement slow, sensual, the air between them crackling with an invisible, electric charge. Her nipples tightened, and the sensitive spot between her legs begged to be touched. His face twisted into a half smile. "Which is it, Stace?"

Damn it. She was a smart, resourceful woman who at the moment was having trouble articulating a thought. She heaved in a deep breath. "I meant you're not interrupting anything."

"That's too bad." His gaze flickered to her mouth.

The haze thickened between them, wrapped around her and tugged. If he knew she'd had her toy out last night thanks to him, that he was the one who'd consumed her thoughts…

"Look, just answer the question, please. What are you doing here?"

"What does it look like I'm doing?"

"Interfering in my life?"

"Protecting you." He stepped back as if he, too, had come to his senses. "Have you forgotten that your boyfriend Cleo's still out there, and he has your key?"

"His name is Leo. And he's no longer my boyfriend." Strangely, that fact didn't seem to bother her half as much as she'd expected it to. Aside from the shock last night, it didn't bother her at all.

"He's not?"

"No."

She shifted from one foot to the other, now acutely aware that she hadn't bothered to throw a robe over her PJs. Proper attire seemed to be the last thing she'd needed to worry about when she'd thought she was about to be murdered, not that she'd ever thought twice about anything she'd worn in front of Grant before. "And much as I hate to admit it, you were right. Thanks to you, he's history."

"Glad you see it that way. For all I knew, the guy was stalking you."

"When I gave him a key? Not that you didn't do the right thing, but what planet are you from anyway, throwing him out? And if you hadn't thrown him out, we wouldn't have…" Stacey licked her lips, last night's play-by-play still fresh on her brain.

"We wouldn't have kissed," he finished, tapping the screwdriver he held against the palm of his hand. "Nothing we can do to change that now." His blue eyes latched onto hers, the look a sensual mix of lust and confusion.

She shivered at the intensity.

So. That kiss was on his brain as much as it was on hers. Still, it meant nothing. Nothing good, anyway.

He broke their gaze, broke the invisible pull between them, and squatted, exchanging the screwdriver for the instructions that came with the new doorknob.

Wow. She should beat a hasty retreat to her bedroom and stay firmly locked in there until he finished. Instead, she did what she'd always done around him while he worked: sat cross-legged somewhere nearby and watched, only this time she surreptitiously set the dildo on the floor behind her. She needed to make sure to give it an extra-thorough cleaning.

She'd never really noticed before, but he had nice hands, and he seemed to know exactly how to touch her, hold her to him, make her believe for one small moment that she was about to step into her happily ever after...

Stacey gave herself a mental shake. Damn. What the hell was wrong with her?

"Look," he said, staring at the instruction sheet. "About that kiss... Let's just forget it ever happened, okay?"

He wanted to forget that kiss? The same one that made her want to, even now, throw herself at him? She breathed out a soft sigh. Did she have a choice? Not unless she wanted to make a fool of herself. "Sure," she finally said, waving one hand dismissively. "Whatever."

"Here." Grant reached for the paper bag beside him. "I brought you a present."

And just like that they'd morphed back to their easygoing style. Really, it was better this way. A whole lot less complicated, anyhow.

She took the bag from him. "You came by last night to give me a present?"

"No. I came to unload." He turned his attention back to the partially opened doorway. "Remind me not to go out with anyone Stephan sets me up with again. What a disaster."

Stephan Porter was one of Grant's partners at Mile High Desert Distillery. But it wasn't Stephan's good looks or playboy charm that captured her attention. Grant had been out on a date last night and it hadn't gone well. Wasn't that just too bad?

*Not.*

She swatted away the twinge of jealousy. "What happened?"

"The usual thing that's wrong with most women: she couldn't stop trying to sell herself instead of just kicking back and relaxing. We were on our first date, for God's sake, and she was practically picking out matching towels."

Stacey handed him the screwdriver at the same time he reached for it. Their fingers brushed, and every ounce of awareness in her shot straight to the surface. She held her breath, traces of electrical charges racing through her, the feeling so foreign, so exquisite, she was almost sure she'd imagined it.

He swallowed and looked away. "Open the bag."

The bag. Right. She peered into it. "Pepper spray?"

"Yeah. I figured since you have an aversion to learning how to handle a gun, this was the next best thing."

A soft warmth filled her and she smiled. It'd be just like Grant to think about pepper spray. "Good idea, but what made you think I needed four of these?"

"One at work, one on your hike, one in your purse, and one in your bedroom." He frowned. "Maybe I should've gotten one for the living room, too."

She whistled. "Pretty thorough, there, Grant." Come to think of it, he was pretty thorough with most things in his life, which probably meant he was pretty thorough in bed, too.

*Easy there, Stace.*

She needed to get a grip before things got way out of hand and she did something really stupid. Like fall for her best friend.

...

*Goddamn, she looks hot as fuck.*

Trying to distract himself by giving her the pepper spray hadn't worked. Nor had focusing on the doorknob like it would explode if he tightened the screws wrong. No matter what he did, Grant couldn't stop illicit thoughts from swirling through his brain. And he sure as hell wished she'd quit staring up at him as she sat cross-legged on the floor. It was bad enough her shorts showed creamy white thighs, but it was what they hid that had his insides in a twist. In this moment, he could honestly admit she was fucking killing him.

"Just remember to keep one with you."

She pulled a pepper spray out and peeled the plastic wrapper off. "Feels easy enough to handle."

Her fingers wrapped around the cylinder in a way that fed Grant's imagination. Coupled with her position on the floor, looking up at him, even the innocent statement had his dick interested. He swallowed, visions of Stacey on her knees in front of him, her mouth working his—

*Fuck.*

*Keep your brain in gear, buddy.*

"Good." He looked away. "That's good."

She crooked up an eyebrow, her expression so adorable he wanted to gather her in his arms, relearn the feel of her on him.

*Double fuck.*

Her gaze landed somewhere behind him. "You do realize it'll cost me a fortune if you change the locks, right? And since I can't afford it, I suggest you change it back."

"Don't worry. I cleared it with the apartment manager." It helped that the two of them were pretty good friends, but Grant still had to pay a hefty fine for violating her rental agreement, *and* he owed the guy a couple bottles of bourbon. But she didn't need to know that.

"You cleared it with him at seven a.m.?"

"Last night."

A corner of her mouth quirked. "That's got to be the most planning I've seen you do in, oh, I don't know…ever."

He scowled. "Maybe I'm turning over a new leaf."

"No need to get so touchy."

Touchy? When had he ever been touchy? He'd learned to roll with life from a pretty young age, so he'd allowed very little to affect him. He wasn't touchy, was he?

He adjusted the knob. The sooner he finished this, the sooner he could blow this place and maybe then he could concentrate on getting his head screwed on straight.

"Grant?"

"Yeah?"

"Why didn't you call before you came over last night?"

"I've never had to before, why would I last night?"

"Good point."

"It's the only kind I make."

She lifted an eyebrow and her gaze narrowed slightly. "So how come you didn't clean up the rose petals before you crawled into my bed?"

"How was I supposed to clean them up? I couldn't run the vacuum in the middle of the night, your neighbors would've been pounding on the door. And I sure as hell wasn't going to pick them up by hand." It was a damned stupid thing to do, throwing rose petals on the floor.

Stacey tilted her head to one side. "And Ariana Grande? Why was her music on?"

"Look, I've had a long week and picked a random playlist because I was too tired to put a movie on. I figured I'd lie down for a bit, but didn't expect to fall asleep." But he *had* fallen asleep, and then Stacey kissed him awake. Kind of like Sleeping Beauty in reverse.

He paused, holding the screwdriver midair. Sleeping Beauty? What the—

Grant hadn't thought of that particular Disney character since he and Stacey were eight and she first dressed up as Sleeping Beauty for Halloween. While he'd refused to go as a Disney prince, her costume had been part of their Halloween tradition for three straight years.

Fuck, he needed to get over it already.

"You free to come to the mayor's brunch with me this Saturday? I'm on official distillery business," he said, latching the last screw in place and securing it.

"This Saturday? But that's your birthday."

"I'm aware of that." He'd realized the two coincided a few days ago, and had to squash the tide of emotion that had been on the verge of letting loose since.

Her tone softened. "You don't have to read the letter this year, you know."

"That's an option." He shrugged. "Who knows what I'll do."

But he did know. As with past birthdays, he'd pull the sheet of lined notebook paper he'd kept all these years from its envelope, smooth out the wrinkles, then read it. Every word. As if he hadn't committed the entire thing to memory and could recite it in his sleep.

Stacey scooted across the floor and put a hand on his arm. "Hey. Your mother loves you, Grant. She did the best she could. She told you so in that letter."

Right. As if the letter that'd been written by his mother when he was eight, then handed to him on his sixteenth birthday by Edward and Miriam Wilson, his last set of foster parents, was supposed to have been enough. Like it was all she needed to do to justify her actions.

"I don't see how lying to an eight-year-old boy, then leaving him in a park with a social worker to be raised in the foster care system shows a mother's love," he gritted out. "Especially when she chose to keep her other son."

"Fair enough," Stacey said, scooting back to her original spot.

He rummaged through the bag of supplies he'd brought with him and tried to shove his past back into the old envelope where it belonged.

As a child, he'd been forced to live in the moment, to accept the curve balls thrown his way and that the future had no certainty. Life had made *that* abundantly clear. Stacey knew this. Which was why she was smart enough to change the subject.

"So how come you're going to the brunch on your birthday?" she asked. "That's not your thing."

"I know." As much as he disliked the idea of shaking hands and smiling at people he didn't really care about, it also meant that he didn't have to put a dime into the distillery to own a part of it. "But it's part of the job now." He glanced in her direction. "So, you coming or not?"

"You could've just *texted* me the invitation."

"I didn't decide until last night. Why text when I knew I'd be here?"

"Oh, right, when you realized you were on a date with a she-devil." She grinned. "Poor Grant needs li'l ol' me to protect him from big, bad, predatory women."

"No, I just wanted to…talk about it," he grumbled. "So will you come or not?"

"Maybe."

He blew out a breath. She hated these things just as much as he did, both of them preferring to be outdoors communing with nature. But there was something in this for her, too. Dinners for Two needed exposure if she was going to make the business really work, and a good portion of the guests that day were her target market. "There'll be a chance to network…"

She sat up straighter, her eyes taking on the excited gleam that never failed to excite *him*. "Well, I have big plans for my business, and meeting new people would definitely help. Of course, that's just the bonus for helping you out…"

Grant chuckled. Yeah, he had her. He just wished she'd let him return the favor. "I still don't get why you think you have to build up your company on your own." He had some extra money, mainly because he didn't need much, which was exactly the way he liked to live his life. "Let me help you."

"Please." She waved him off. "That's cheating and you know it."

He eyed her from the top of her tousled brown hair to her purple and pink painted toenails. Amazing how she could morph from girl-next-door cute to sexy as fuck. He beat the thought back. "Look, we're friends. Friends take care of each other. What's so wrong with that?"

"Nothing. But you know I can't take it. All four of my sisters made it without anyone's help. Why should I be any different?"

She had a ton of determination, he'd give her that. "Let me know if you change your mind."

"You know something?" she said, tilting her head to one side. "It's so hard to stay pissed at you."

"You can't help it. I'm adorable." He grinned and attached a screw. "You also know I'm right."

She gave him a long-suffering sigh. "Why aren't you taking the woman you were out with a couple of weeks ago? What was her name? Lucy?"

"Jill."

She frowned. "Which one was Lucy?"

"She's long gone. And, yeah, no way am I taking Jill with me. As soon as she found out I was a part owner at the distillery, she was practically planning our wedding." He grimaced. That would never happen.

Not that women wanted to hear stuff like that, which was why he tended to keep his relationships brief. In the end, this worked out best for everyone.

"Right. Commitment issues."

This was what he liked most about Stacey. She never judged, and simply accepted him for who he was. The way he figured it, Stacey and his foster brother Aidan were the only people who knew everything about him and still stuck by his side, and even then, Aidan kind of had to stick around. Stacey didn't have any familial obligation to him, and yet she hadn't walked away like everyone else he'd stupidly let into his life.

"So are you coming or not? There's bound to be some eligible bachelors there, too. You know, since Cleo wasn't 'the one.'"

He said the words but a part of him protested at the thought. What a dumb-ass. Stacey deserved her shot at finding her idea of Mr. Perfect, so if that guy was at this shindig, then she should have at him.

Because as much as he wanted to kiss Stacey again to see if he'd dreamed up the chemistry between them, losing her wasn't worth it.

# Chapter Four

For the umpteenth time Stacey glanced at her phone. Where was Grant? She frowned. A better question was why was she concerned? The guy was always late to Therapy Tuesday. This shouldn't feel any different.

She sipped from the Chinese teacup and glanced outside the restaurant window. This late in the afternoon, a blanket of crisp, chilled air had replaced the pockets of sunshine, and the fact summer was almost here was the only reason butterflies had taken up residence in the pit of her stomach. That's all it was.

In the distance, the top of Chinaman Hat was shrouded in the glow of the setting sun. Rays of light bounced off the mountain's slightly rounded peak. Maybe her offering hadn't helped with the Leo situation, but surely it'd work eventually? It had worked for Aidan Ross, Grant's foster brother, and it'd worked for her sister, Carly, too. Both examples added to the claims of others in the area who'd sworn they, too, had found their one true love.

She might still be waiting, but there had to be *something*

to it.

Grant slid into the seat across from her and reached for her hand. "Sorry I'm late."

How come she never noticed how hot he looked when he smiled? Or how good his hand felt on hers when he squeezed it in greeting? He'd done it countless times before, only this time her heart hammered and she was left fighting like hell to bring it under control.

"You say that like it's the first time instead of a weekly thing." Thank God her voice was steady. Carefully, she set her cup down and reached for the teapot.

"Hey, Therapy Tuesday's supposed to be laid-back," he protested as she poured his tea. "This is cheaper than real therapy, remember? Besides, when have I ever *not* shown up?"

Steam wafted out of his cup. "Yeah, yeah." She pushed it toward him and set the teapot down. "Lucky for you this isn't an official therapy session. I'd be charging you extra for being late all the time."

He snorted. "Like you haven't kept me hanging, too."

"Oh, please. I've rearranged my work schedule to be here every week."

Their weekly dinner at The Chinese Stop was their answer to long workdays and bad dates. It was a chance to touch base with each other, and, honestly, was something Stacey looked forward to. Sometimes they'd even head back to her place for a movie, complete with popcorn and a bowl of miniature candy bars.

Her cheeks flamed at the memory of the last time Grant was in her bed, at the way she'd kissed him, straddled him, all set to…

Yeah, a movie was probably not something she should plan on tonight. In fact, they should probably stay away from her bed altogether. At least for a little while.

Stacey tapped her open menu, determined to bring their friendship back onto firmer ground. "Are you going for the duck or the special? Mei-Ling swears the special tonight is particularly good."

Right on cue, the Chinese hostess appeared at their table. "She right," she said, lifting her chin in Stacey's direction. "The special is good."

Grant looked dubious. "Can't you give us a hint? One tiny hint?"

"No." Mei-Ling clucked as she wiped at a spot on the dark table. The dragon-shaped ornamental pin at the top of her perfectly coiffed hair shone in the shaft of afternoon light. "You know my son. He say special just that. Special. He make whatever he want when someone order. You order before. It's good." She nodded her head as if willing Grant to admit it was good.

"It was, but I don't know. I've had enough adventure this week," he muttered, reaching for the battered menu off to one side.

"I can relate." Stacey had definitely had a bunch of memories in the surprise column the past few days, but that didn't mean she wasn't up for a couple more. "But I'll take the special." She stared at Grant. "And if you're good, I'll give you a bite."

"I'll end up with half of it, anyway. Same as always."

"You aren't complaining, are you?"

"Of course not." He looked a tad offended.

"Didn't think so."

"I'll take the number five combination," he said, closing the menu.

Mei-Ling chuckled. "When you two gonna marry?"

Stacey nearly choked. To cover her reaction, she grabbed her cup and took a sip, the tea burning its way down her throat.

"Well," Grant drawled. "I imagine that Stacey will get married when she finds 'the one.'"

"Hey." She frowned as she cradled the teacup in her hands. "There's nothing wrong with searching for the right guy."

"There is if it means dating idiots like Cleo."

"Leo."

"Whatever." Grant went back to studying the menu like he hadn't already ordered.

Stacey shot the hostess a small smile. "And I imagine Grant's never gonna tie himself to a woman." For more reasons than one, but she decided to keep it light. "You never know when one will expect him to at least know how to boil water. Which, come to think of it, is most women. Judging from his cooking skills so far, he's not going to find anyone anytime soon."

"Oh yeah? Dennis teach you." Mei-Ling pointed across the crowded restaurant toward the kitchen. "He very good."

Grant smiled and leaned forward, capturing Stacey's gaze. "You can't cook, either. Maybe that's why you haven't found him yet."

"I can, too." She straightened in her seat. "I just don't do it a lot."

"Whatever." He raised his head and waggled his brows at the older woman. "But if I learned how to cook, or heaven forbid, found a woman to cook for me, I wouldn't come here very much, and that means I wouldn't get to see you, Mei-Ling."

Stacey rolled her eyes and held up a hand to shield her face from him. "Not gonna happen," she said to the older woman in a stage whisper, pointing in his direction with her free hand. "Commitment issues."

Mei-Ling laughed, the sound pure and strong even in the noise surrounding them. "Like you two already married."

She shook her head and walked away, her thin frame belying the strength that emanated from her. "I get this going for you," she said over one shoulder. "You relax."

The satisfaction Stacey felt soon disappeared when she caught the sexy half smile on Grant's face. A thrill shot through her and she breathed in deeply, biting down on her lower lip.

Relax.

Right.

...

When *was* he going to settle down?

Before the other night, with Stacey, it'd have been an emphatic *never*. Now...

Grant frowned. What the hell was he thinking? It was *still* a never.

He glanced at his best friend as she stared out the window and sipped her tea. The woman might be petite, but she had balls of steel and didn't mind taking on people and situations way bigger than she was. She was also obstinate about finding some perfect guy, a fact that annoyed the hell out of him. That kind of love wasn't realistic or guaranteed, so why bust your ass trying to find something that might not exist?

The hell of it was, as much as she obsessed over finding "the one," he wouldn't change a damn thing about her. No, as far as he was concerned, Stacey was perfect.

His attention was drawn to her hands when she set her teacup down. Even now he remembered the way they skimmed over his body the other night... He gave himself a mental shake. Why relive something that'd only torture his dick?

"Julian wants a dinner at Chinaman Hat," she said absently. "Soon, he said. I wonder if it'll be too cold for him?"

"Let me guess," he said smoothly. "Julian's your new boyfriend." The words came out easily, but felt...wrong. He frowned. Wrong because she'd just broken up with Cleo/Leo the other night. Otherwise, he didn't give a rip as long as she was happy. He smothered the taunting voice in his head that insisted the whole thing was a load of bull.

"Unless you think I'm desperate enough to pursue a nearly octogenarian who, by the way, has been happily married for sixty years, then sure." The corners of her mouth lifted slightly, and he couldn't seem to tear his gaze away. She had full lips, pouty lips, and damn if he didn't want another taste. "But, sadly, I don't think Julian would trade Martha for someone like me."

He sucked in a deep breath and forced his brain into gear. "Sixty years? Do people really still stay together that long?"

"They're living proof. Anyway, Julian's one of my best clients." She leaned forward, her eyes lighting up. "He's been with me since I quit my waitress job at the resort last year, and he's been pimping Dinners for Two to everyone he knows. He's better than any ad I could place."

Dinners for Two. He understood the concept behind it—putting together romantic dinners for guys who didn't have a clue how to impress a woman on their own—he just didn't get *why*. What kind of guy made such a big fuss over planning a simple *meal*? Grant preferred throwing a couple of steaks on the grill or ordering takeout. Both were easy to execute, and both tasted pretty good.

Still, he nodded but said nothing. That was the beauty of their relationship. He didn't have to make small talk, didn't have to fill voids in conversation with her. She made everything easy. And he'd fight damn hard to make sure none of that changed.

"He sent a text just before you got here. He wants to meet to discuss the next few dinners, but he wants the very next one at Chinaman Hat." She sighed, the sound soft and wistful and very feminine. "So romantic."

He narrowed his gaze. "I never could understand why people consider it romantic. It's a hunk of rock. Great for climbing, hiking, and biking, sure. But romantic?"

"It's the story behind it, silly."

He shook his head. "Some mythical Chinese dude treks over the Pacific Ocean, settles here, and falls in love with a local. Refuses to go back to China and tells his dad that he'd just as soon stay here as a rock than leave the woman behind. Then *poof,* he ends up a rock." He snorted. "Who's dumb enough to believe that a guy'd do that? Let alone the whole rock thing."

"Apparently, not you." She sat up and pierced him with a hard stare.

"You're such a dreamer."

"I'm a *romantic*. I believe in two people finding happiness in each other."

"Is that why you focus so much energy on finding your prince charming? Why you read all those relationship blogs and watch YouTube videos?" He'd never thought about it before, but now he was curious. "Because that's the only way for you to be happy?"

"I never said it was the only way." She bit her lower lip, a sure sign that the cogs were turning in her brain, and her face took on a dreamy look as she stared off in the distance. "But finding the right guy to spend my life with…it's something I've always wanted for myself, something deep and meaningful that'd make life larger and brighter and fulfilling. You know, like what happens on the Hallmark Channel movies."

Holy fuck, she was serious. "That's a lot of pressure to hang on one guy. Kind of stifling, really."

She blew out a breath and frowned. "What's so wrong about finding someone you just click with?"

"Not a damn thing." He wanted to point out that the two of them clicked, that they had something deep and meaningful, but something stopped him. The last thing he wanted to do was lead her on. That'd make him the worst kind of jerk, not to mention ruin something he considered pretty damned amazing.

He stared at her over the rim of his teacup, and by the time he set it down, he knew he couldn't keep his mouth shut. It'd probably cost him, but what the hell? "You have your act together better than a lot of women I know. You don't need to find some guy to make you what you already are—perfect."

She blinked at him. "Um, wow. Thanks, Grant."

"You're welcome."

"You two still fighting?" Mei-Ling set a couple of steaming plates in front of them. "You marry, I tell you."

Grant shook himself out of the soft way Stacey was looking at him and waved Me-Ling off. "Yeah, yeah. I'll marry her when fortune cookies grow on trees."

"You wanna tree? Dennis could make. He make all the fortune cookies here, too. He hang from tree." She made a motion with both hands, showing a cookie hanging from a branch, by the looks of it.

Stacey's eyes lingered on him a moment longer, but then she smiled up at the woman. "His cookies are the best, Mei-Ling," she said. "I can't wait to read what words of wisdom he's got for us today."

Her smile was radiant, reaching across the table and tugging at Grant's chest.

He gave himself a mental shake. Radiant? What the *fuck* was wrong with him?

She inhaled deeply and glanced down at her plate. "This looks great, by the way. I'm glad I ordered it."

"Trust me," the older woman said, reaching for the teapot and refilling their cups. "I know what you like." She set the pot down. "You two, you like each other. You gonna marry."

Something about the whole exchange settled uneasily on Grant. It was dumb. There wasn't any doubt that he loved Stacey, would do anything for her. But marriage to anyone? Definitely not until fortune cookies grew on trees.

# Chapter Five

Stacey stared at Julian Howe's crinkled face. The living room they were in, complete with baby grand piano, faded to black. All that registered was the old man's smile, so incongruous with the bombshell he'd dropped. How could he possibly be so calm?

"You're dying?" she whispered. Pain stabbed through her chest, constricting her heart while her brain processed what he'd just told her. He was dying.

It wasn't possible. No way. No. Way.

He was one of the liveliest people she'd ever met. He had a lot of energy for his age. Well, okay, so he'd slowed down the last couple of months, but it hadn't appeared to be anything serious.

She searched his face, sure she hadn't heard him right. He always had a ready smile and a kind word. How could life be so cruel? Leaning forward, she swallowed back the lump in her throat. "Are you sure?"

"Afraid so." He shrugged. "It does happen to the best of us, you know."

She leaned back and scanned him from the top of his balding head to the plaid slippers on his feet. "You look fine to me. Maybe the doctors are wrong? Did you get a second opinion?"

"Why, thank you. I feel pretty good right now." The man's smile broadened. "But, yes, my dear. I got a second opinion, and a third, even. The cancer's spread so that I've only a few weeks left at most."

He reached out, then, his cold fingers registering when he patted her hand. "That's why I need to make sure Martha and I share these dinners more frequently, see. I want to give her these last memories of how much I love her, how much I cherish her, how I'll cherish her even after I'm gone. Can you understand that?"

His gentle words, softly spoken, pierced through Stacey until she wasn't sure she could handle the painful pressure. But she had to. If not for her, then most definitely for the man she'd come to recognize as a friend.

"Understand?" she finally said, swallowing the lump in her throat. "Of course I do." How often had she wished for that kind of love from someone? A love so deep and everlasting it made her heart ache? "I'm going to make sure you have the best, most romantic dinners I've ever created. I'll even get with Carly and put together a special menu, if you like."

"You always plan the nicest evenings. It's why Martha and I enjoy Dinners for Two so much."

The praise warred with her sinking heart. But, in the face of his illness, she wasn't going to bring him down.

She stared at the lively gray-blue eyes of her favorite client. He seemed fine, but she didn't want him to overdo it, either. "Are you sure you're okay to travel to the different locations you wanted? I mean, are you sure you aren't in any pain or anything? We can rethink the venues, you know."

"Bah." He dropped her hand and waved her off. "Don't worry about me. Frankly, nothing would be more painful to me than not giving this to Martha."

This. *This* was what her heart longed for, to have someone love her enough to plan a special evening that she'd always remember. She stuffed down the pang in her chest and the lump in her throat that threatened to overwhelm her. Breathing in deeply, she tried for a smile instead. "That's lovely."

He sat back in the wingback chair, a blanket over his legs, and stared into space, then turned his head just far enough to capture her gaze. "Did I ever tell you that the first moment I laid eyes on her was in a crowded restaurant? I didn't know what hit me, but it was like a jolt of some sort, almost like God was talking to me. That's when I knew." He swallowed. "I knew in that moment that I was going to marry her."

He sighed. "You might not realize it now, as young as you are, but it goes too quickly, Stacey. Too quickly."

What the hell was she supposed to say to that? There wasn't a damn thing that came to mind that didn't sound like a platitude, yet she felt the intensity of the moment as if it were her own, felt the beauty that flowed from him as he spoke of his one true love.

One day she'd share a deep love with someone so that sixty years together would pass too quickly for both of them. The longing in her chest deepened. She'd waited long enough for "one day." Really, it needed to show up soon.

"My only regret," he continued softly, breaking into her thoughts, "is that I didn't make her half as happy as she's made me." He cleared his throat again, grabbed the arms of the chair, then pulled himself forward. "That's why I want everything to be perfect. You can do that for me, can't you?"

"Absolutely."

*No pressure, right?*

She stared into Julian's kind eyes and willed every ounce of strength to the surface. No matter how horrible the situation was, she had to keep it together. Besides, if Julian wasn't falling apart, then who the hell was she to do so?

Stacey bit her lower lip and fumbled in her purse for a pen. "Well, then, we'd better get started on the menu, huh?"

...

Crowds sucked. Unless it was at a football game or something. But some frou-frou event with free champagne and bite-size food that looked like it belonged in an entertainment magazine—not to mention the suit he was forced to wear? Grant hated the entire thing even if it did benefit the distillery.

*One event down, one to go...* In the immediate future, anyway. When summer rolled around he'd been warned there'd be more publicity stuff to do.

He huffed out a breath. The mayor's brunch was an important event that funded various educational programs. The place was full of some of the top business owners and local investors who supported the majority of Milestone's charities, and now he got to hang with them. Oh, yay.

A jazz quartet blasted out a fast-paced tune in a corner of the room where some attendees danced. Not his taste in music, but to be fair, things could've been worse. There could've been no music at all. He stood at the edge of the rows that marked the silent auction tables. Beside them people were elbow to elbow, busy bidding on a variety of packages.

With the money raised this afternoon, the local library hoped to stock more children's books, and the local high school planned to extend the sports program to low-income youth in the areas surrounding Milestone. Both were worthy of support.

Which was why he was happy to have pulled the trigger

and put in the final bid for a couple of kayaks. Sure, he paid full price, but it was for a good cause.

He raised the champagne flute to his lips, the letter feeling like a lead weight in his jacket pocket. In a twisted way it seemed fitting that he carry it on his first official role as company spokesperson. The letter kept things real, the reminder plain. Live the moment because tomorrow, his whole world could disappear.

He schooled his face into what he hoped was an interested stare as he scanned the rest of the ballroom. He had to admit, it was a good turnout. If it were up to him, though, he'd have happily spent the day mountain biking with Stacey. Or maybe watching some action-adventure flick with a bowl of popcorn on her—

Yeah, maybe they'd have to skip the whole Netflix thing for a while. God knew he couldn't climb into her bed again without remembering the last time he was in it.

He glanced over at his companion, and admired the sleeveless, form-hugging peach cocktail dress she wore. Paired with heels, the outfit made her smooth, bare legs seem longer, somehow. He sucked in a deep breath and blew it out slowly. At least she was here today. He just hoped she didn't feel weird being back at the place where she used to wait tables for the people she now mingled with.

If anything, it made him proud of all she'd accomplished since quitting.

"If I had a say in things, I'd have done a pairing instead," she said from beside him. "You know, maybe a beer, wine, and spirits tasting so guests could see how each one complements the food. Or a mimosa bar paired with different brunch items."

"As long as it's not fish bait–size, I could go for that."

"Maybe even a brunch built around tapas… You know, for an international twist."

He smiled. Her brain was at it, taking ideas from the event to use in her own business. That was the thing about Stacey—she could run a business and seemingly be working all the time, but for her it was fun, too.

"If *I* had a say, we'd be doing this outdoors instead, something that'd focus on the natural beauty of the area." He frowned. "We'd probably all be freezing our asses off, though."

"That's why portable heaters exist, my friend." She tapped him on the arm, and warmth traveled from the point of contact to the rest of his body. "What's wrong with the resort?" she asked while his brain was still trying to process the whole warmth thing.

"Other than it's stuffy?"

She rolled her eyes and looked around at the walls. He wondered what she found so fascinating with gold trim and heavy curtains.

"It's been here since Milestone was founded," she said. "Sure, it's been remodeled since, but it's got history to it. If these walls could talk, imagine how many proposals were said or first dates were had or anniversaries celebrated."

"What a romantic."

"I've never pretended to be anything else." She sighed and smiled up at him in a way that made him itch to hold her, itch to have her in his arms again. The battle warred inside him, and a crackling sensation whipped through his body, urging him to give in, to pull her toward him, consequences be damned.

Her brown eyes captured his, and the room disappeared. "Grant?"

His name was a question and a promise, and it was all he could do to hang onto some shred of self-control. He held out his half-filled glass of champagne. "I'm done with this. Let's get something else."

And just like that, the world invaded again. Laughter registered from a nearby table. A saxophone blared a solo.

"Let me see that." She raised an eyebrow and handed the glass of champagne back. "It's warm. You've been nursing this the whole time?"

"Not a fan." He turned. "I'd rather have some bourbon."

"There's a surprise."

She looped her arm through his as they walked. It wasn't like she hadn't ever done such a thing before, but damn, it felt good to at least touch her.

"Three o'clock, man your stations," she said.

Code for heads-up, someone or something of interest was in the area, and play along if necessary. Grant casually glanced in the direction she indicated. He lasered in on the guy and immediately recognized one of the newest members of the elite eligible bachelors' pool. It helped to ride the coattails of a wealthy family.

Not that Grant had had any experience in that department.

"Todd just moved to Milestone," Stacey said, untangling her arm from his. "I'm going to introduce myself." Her hips swayed slightly as she walked, lengthening the distance between them, but he stood rooted while his brain clicked backward to another time, another place, another Todd.

The last time he'd seen his younger brother, the little guy was four. And he knew their mother had taken Todd far from Milestone with no plans to return.

Grant placed a hand on his jacket, over his heart where the letter was safely tucked. The familiar pang arced through him, gripped his chest in a vise that seemed to tighten further. The stab of pain was expected, the tumbling memories were not. He tried to stop them, tried to stuff them back where they belonged, but they persisted.

The miniature racecar he'd left in his seat when his mother had unlocked the rear passenger door to let him out at the park that day. Todd crying when their mother drove away. The confusion Grant felt as he chased after them until someone had grabbed him by the collar. It was the social worker he later discovered his mother had been in contact with. The one she'd *planned* to leave him with.

Though the foster care system gave him the basics, he knew that eventually nothing was permanent. Not his room, his toys, and definitely not the families he'd thought would never leave.

He sucked in another deep breath to ease the pain. It was a long time ago. A lifetime ago.

Time to control his thoughts, to divert them to Edward and Miriam Wilson, the foster parents who *had* kept him, then to Aidan, and finally to Stacey.

His gaze followed his companion, who was now talking with the guy.

Stacey. Her sweetness. Her kindness. Both conveyed in her smile.

Stacey. The way she took the world with both hands, the way she made her life her own and didn't apologize to anyone for it.

Stacey. His rock in an otherwise dizzyingly crazy world.

The memories slowed, then stopped. *Fina-fucking-ly.*

By the time he reached her she was engrossed in deep conversation with the guy, and turned just as he approached. "Hey, you know Todd Schoonover, don't you?"

"Hey, man." The younger man raised his chin. "Heard a lot about you. We should get together sometime."

"Welcome to Milestone." Grant clasped the extended hand, then took Stacey's champagne glass from her. "I'll take care of this for you."

"Sure. We'll be right here."

He nodded but knew he wouldn't be back for her anytime soon. She was either working a deal or chatting the guy up to see if he was a potential Mr. Right. No way was he interrupting.

So how come leaving her there literally felt like he'd lost his best friend?

He heaved in a deep breath. It was her job to network, to make connections that could launch her business to the next level. It was *his* job to do the same thing for the distillery. It was in both their interests to remember that. So there wasn't a problem, right?

He had no claim on her, and some of the guys she'd dated over the years were even ones he'd given the thumbs-up to. No denying that something was different, though...

*They'd kissed.*

So what?

*And she'd rubbed up against him.*

She didn't know it was him.

*And he'd liked it.*

Goddamn it. There was no good comeback to that one. But it didn't change the fact that it was an honest-to-goodness mistake. One that now had him reduced to arguing with himself like a teenage girl, for God's sake.

*Snap out of it, dude.*

When it came down to it, being her best friend was his only place in her life. Which was why he was focused on her now.

He ditched the champagne glasses on an empty table and turned.

"Hello, Grant." Richard Banks stepped in front of him and stuck out his hand. His grip was firm, sure, and filled with the kind of authority that came from years in political office, despite the man bun that gave him a distinctly youthful appearance. "Looks like this fundraiser is on track to beat last year's numbers. Thanks for participating."

"Thanks for the invitation." No one with an ounce of

sense said no to Milestone's mayor, especially if one owned a fledgling business the way Grant now did. "The distillery would be happy to participate next year, too."

Inside, he cringed at the thought. But as the official face of the company, he had to do whatever he could to keep the distillery in front of the public, right?

"I've heard about you, about the different blends you've created. Quite impressive."

Grant felt his face heat. For all the accolades he'd earned over the years, he couldn't shake the feeling that he was always on the edge, always being judged and on the verge of being found lacking. "Yeah, well, the spirits market is pretty competitive. Gotta innovate to stay ahead of the crowd, you know."

"Bah." The older man grinned. "No need to be modest. Just keep turning out an award-winning bourbon and you'll be fine." He lowered his voice. "My wife wants to know the secret to your Moose Mile blend."

Wasn't an award-winning bourbon what every master distiller aimed for? Grant swallowed. "Well, that particular blend has seven spices and brown sugar in it." Personally, it was too sweet for his taste, but market analysis showed that middle-aged women like the mayor's wife loved it. "We bottled just forty cases of it this year." Which also meant that they could sell it at a premium.

"She swears it's her favorite. Like drinking dessert." He gave a short laugh. "You know what they say: if the wife's happy, everybody's happy."

"Right." Grant had definitely had a few foster mothers who fit that description.

He shook off the reminder. His job was to sell the distillery to the public, and if the mayor's wife liked a particular blend, all the better for the business. "If there's more of a demand for it, I'll increase production."

There. That sounded professional.

Of course, he'd have to make sure they put out some fancy marketing plan if he did increase production, but if things continued, Moose Mile could end up being the blend that bumped the distillery up to the next level.

He looked around the room again, searching for a glimpse of Stacey. Nothing. He'd only been gone a few minutes—had she taken off? Worse, gone home with one of the guys she'd chatted up? Maybe even that Todd guy? Sure, it was only the middle of the day, but still…

Grant clenched his teeth. Why was he even thinking about this? Stacey was an intelligent woman, free to sleep with whomever she chose.

"Grant?"

The mayor's voice cut through his thoughts, and brought him squarely back to the present. "I'm sorry." He let out an apologetic laugh. "I wondered where my date ended up." Should he call her his date? This wasn't really a date, was it? "Stacey Winters. I think you know her father? Winters Construction?"

"Yes, I know Stacey. She's got a reputation for being quite a pistol, that one." He shook his head dismissively. "I imagine any man would have his hands full with her."

Huh? What the hell was that supposed to mean? He frowned at the amusement on the mayor's lips and fought the need to defend his friend. Who the hell cared what anyone thought about her? "I need to find her. If you'll excuse me?"

"Of course."

He wove his way through the crowd to where he'd left Stacey, but the various interruptions along the way took him longer than he'd have liked. He fought down the irritation, fought down the irrational need to ignore city council members and the head of the local chamber of commerce.

*This is my job.*

Besides, it wasn't like he needed to do more than make small talk with any of them. The reminder wound through his head and was the only thing that stopped him from pushing through the crowd.

By the time he'd reached the spot where he'd left her, she still hadn't returned. Probably continuing her manhunt. He shoved a hand into the front pocket of his suit pants and casually looked around. If she hadn't already left, there were a couple places she could've gone. Either toward the gardens or toward the resort's pool area.

Back when she'd waited tables here, the gardens were her old stomping grounds. He'd sometimes met her on her breaks there, where they'd spend time staring at the sky as she planned her next move. The garden was where she'd first told him about Dinners for Two, and she'd been so excited about it that he couldn't help but feel excited for her.

That was the thing about Stacey. No matter where she was in life, she was always planning her next move. He, on the other hand, was perfectly content to let life happen. If they were anything more than friends, they'd drive each other crazy, so the whole world-stopping buzz thing had to end.

A splash of peach at the edge of the dance floor caught his attention. It was a slow song, and she was dancing with Todd. Grant continued to focus on Stacey, on the smile on her face and the way she gracefully moved to the beat of the music. Those dance lessons she'd taken when they were kids had obviously paid off.

Something deep, something primal, bubbled to the surface. His gaze was sharply focused on the pair as he made his way to the center of the dance floor, and before he knew it, he'd tapped Todd on the shoulder.

When the man turned, Grant stifled the urge to pull him off of her. "May I cut in?" he asked instead, his eyes fixed on Stacey.

She opened her mouth slightly. Was that relief on her face?

God, he wanted to kiss her. So much so that he held himself rigid to keep from acting on impulse. There was no denying that an unexplainable *something* sizzled through his veins, sizzled between them.

"Of course," she answered. "Thanks again for the dance, Todd. Good talking to you."

The other man released her, then nodded. "I'll call you."

Without a word, Grant gathered her into his arms and held her close, her head right beneath his chin, and her body pressed against him just hard enough so he could feel her softness. The scent of lemons wafted off of her, and he breathed in deeply.

How could something like a simple slow dance feel so… right?

Shit.

It wasn't like they hadn't danced together before. She'd been the one to teach him when Grant was afraid he'd humiliate himself at their first school dance. While he'd rolled his eyes at the time, secretly pleased he had her around to help, he had to admit that holding her now felt good. *Too* damn good.

He took another deep breath, then moved his head to one side of hers so he wouldn't have to shout over the music.

*Right. Keep telling yourself that.*

"What's going on, Grant?" she asked in his ear. "You've been edgy since we got here."

He nearly groaned at the warmth of her breath against his cheek, and hoped like hell she didn't feel him shudder. Stacey was his person, the first to be a part of his small tribe. He'd known her even longer than Aidan. Grant and Aidan had both been through the foster care system, and both had come out of it in pretty good shape, but Stacey would always be his first.

He tightened his arms around her, swallowing while his pulse raced and blood pounded in his ears. Risking something like their friendship was insane, especially when he had no idea how she felt. Still, he settled on the truth before he could talk himself out of it. "I could get lost in your eyes."

# Chapter Six

*I could get lost in your eyes.*

If he was going for the shock factor, it worked. Stacey bit down on her lower lip. Was he serious? She couldn't tell. This was Grant, for heaven's sake. He didn't say stuff like that. Ever. But she couldn't help but wonder if she really *did* have that effect on him.

Almost afraid of what she'd see, she glanced up at him—and caught the flash of regret that crossed his face.

Oh.

She tried to come up with something to say that wouldn't make the situation more awkward. "That's, uh…that's a good line, Grant."

*That's it. Keep it light, keep it friendly. Don't let him see how much you wish he'd meant it.*

"Not if it's true," he said, waggling his eyebrows.

Which in Grant terms meant he hadn't intended the compliment to come out sounding serious. "Funny guy," she said, even as a pang of regret, followed immediately by a surge of longing, swept through her. She shoved both aside.

He grinned. "That's me. Hope you didn't mind me cutting in."

"Are you gonna police who I dance with now? Really, Grant, what's next? A chastity belt?"

Like she needed one of those. It'd been ages since she'd had sex.

He cleared his throat. "Hey, it's none of my business who you dance with, but you know what is?"

"What?"

"Making sure you're having a good time. You know, since I dragged you here and everything."

Oh, well, okay. That she could believe. "I've made some promising business contacts, and even have a couple of events planned."

"What about the manhunt?"

She leaned back and scowled at him. "Would you quit calling it that?"

"Why? That's pretty much what it is, right? A hunt for 'the one.'" He batted his eyelashes at her.

"Goofball." Stacey laughed, then frowned. He kind of had a point. When she agreed to be his plus one, she'd harbored hope that she'd run into the guy for her.

And that's when the realization struck her like she was a pin at the end of a bowling lane. She might have hoped to meet her special someone, but she'd been so distracted by Grant that she hadn't even bothered to consider which of the eligible men here might be worth talking to.

She froze as the thought deepened, strengthened. Her breathing shallowed and she fought like the devil to figure out why she'd allowed her best friend in the whole wide universe to distract her. Tilting her head, she searched Grant's blue eyes, their color unexpected on someone with dark hair. She could get lost in *his* eyes—*had* gotten lost a time or two just this week.

He scanned her face and frowned, then leaned forward. "Let's get out of here."

She felt his breath when he whispered in her ear, sending bolts of electricity through her. Every nerve was on hyperalert, every cell at the ready. For what, she wasn't quite sure. After all, it wasn't like he'd suggested they get a room or anything.

He guided her off the dance floor and toward a side door, then held her hand as they stepped outside the stifling room. Heaters dotted the terrace, providing respite from the cool air, in spite of the midday sun. This had always been a beautiful spot, one of her favorite places at the resort, even in winter.

"Here." He shrugged out of his suit jacket and draped it over her shoulders. "You've got to be freezing."

"Thanks." The captured heat from his body seeped into hers, warming her and melding with her own sizzling, slow heat. She gulped in a deep breath, tried her damnedest to still her pounding heart. He gave her his jacket. So what? It was what a gentleman did, and Grant was definitely a gentleman.

The sound of water splashing from the large fountain in the back gardens played a soothing background to the muffled music seeping through the closed ballroom doors. The whole scene was magical, romantic, even—with the right guy.

He reached for her hand again, effectively turning her until she faced him fully. His gaze pierced hers, his smile made her heart pound. Or maybe it was the gentle circles he made with his thumb on the back of her hand.

"You okay?"

"Yeah." She nodded. "It was getting stuffy in there."

"In more ways than one."

He was right. In the past they'd have made an appearance, bowed out at the earliest opportunity, and made a beeline for the mountains or the lake or the river, or maybe even…

Netflix.

She swallowed. *Think of something to say.* Something that'd break this spell he seemed to have cast over her.

With her free hand, she tugged the jacket tighter around her and felt the envelope in the breast pocket. It had to be the letter from his mom. "Did you read it yet?" Knowing him, he'd read the letter at least once, probably more.

He stared at something beyond her left shoulder. "I read it this morning."

"That's good." She nodded. "Any new insights?"

This was a conversation they had every year, dissecting what his mother might've been trying to convey through her words. Sure, they were written a long time ago, and she was likely a very different person now, but who really knew? It wasn't like the woman had tried to reach out to Grant, had tried to make up for the years since she'd abandoned him.

"No." He blew out a breath. "Same as always. Lots of questions and no answers."

When they'd first met, he'd been the new kid at her school, alone and afraid. All she'd known was that he'd been dropped off at a park to play while his mother took off with his younger brother. What kind of a woman abandoned her kid? Let alone one as cool as Grant?

She squeezed his hand tight, but when she tried to let go, he held on. Fine with her. She stepped close and gave him a hug.

Life could be so brutally unfair. Grant. Julian and Martha. Her own inability to find love. Really, was it too much to ask that life *be* fair?

Truthfully, she'd tried not to think about the old man, or his disease, or the fact that his last few weeks would be spent planning the perfect dinners for him to share with his wife.

"I learned something about Julian this week," she said. "He's sick."

Grant pulled back, his eyebrows up, his gaze searching hers. "I'm guessing it's more serious than that, right?" His tone was even, calm, and affected her in a way that made her know he really cared, too.

She nodded. And that's when the ache she'd held at bay for most of the day spilled out of her in a mash of sorrow with a sprinkle of anxiety. Stacey reluctantly turned away from him, from his heat, and leaned against the balcony rail, one hand gripping onto the cold metal for support. "How could someone so kind and loving and giving have to go through something as horrible as cancer? It's just not fair."

"I know it isn't."

For the first time since she'd left Julian's house, tendrils of doubt snaked in. "He wants me to plan all these perfect dinners for him and Martha. What if I can't do it, Grant? What if I'm not good enough?"

"Oh, please, you're going to be great."

"But what if I'm not?" She was pretty good at functioning under pressure, good at keeping her emotions at bay, no matter how badly she wanted to ugly-cry, but at the moment, she was failing miserably.

It's not that she'd never bawled in front of Grant before. He'd been the one whose shoulder she'd cried on when little Tommy Roberts pulled her hair in the third grade and she'd gotten in trouble for giving him a black eye. But there was something different about this time, something more personal, more intimate.

"Hey." He stepped toward her, stopping so they stood less than a foot apart. "Don't tell me you've taken that all on yourself."

She blinked up at him. "What do you mean?"

"You're putting too much pressure on yourself. You're good at what you do, so just keep doing it."

"I know that. It's just that…it's so…*sad*." Her heart ached and she eased in a deep breath to keep from falling off into some sort of weird emotional abyss.

"You have a big heart, no doubt about that. But think about it, Stace. You're kind of helping them keep their relationship alive. It's another moment for them, another memory."

"You and your moments." She shook her head and smiled.

He shrugged. "Each moment is all we really have, right? Can't live in the past, and the future…" He shrugged. "Well, you can't bank on any sort of a future."

He'd always had this view on life, likely because of his past. She stared into his eyes, blue pools so mysterious, yet so inviting. She breathed deeply, filling her lungs with as much oxygen as she could. God, he smelled good, too. Spicy. Was that a new cologne or something? How come she hadn't noticed it before?

"Stace?"

"Yeah?"

"You zoned on me there for a sec. You okay?"

"Of course I'm okay. And I didn't zone on you."

A small smile curled his mouth. "Then answer the question."

Well, shit. He totally got her there. She could fake it, but what would be the point? "Fine. What question?"

He closed the gap between them, reaching a hand out to move a few strands of hair from her face. A shiver chased through her at the light contact. "Would you like me to take you home?"

"With you?"

Oh, shit. Did she really ask that?

His eyes widened a fraction, a gleam of interest reflected in them before they shuttered, effectively keeping her from knowing for sure. "You want to go home with me?" he asked carefully.

What the hell? She'd opened the door, so to speak. And technically he started it with his ridiculous comment about getting lost in her eyes. Would it be so bad, letting him comfort her in whatever way he saw fit? And maybe…hopefully… more? "I mean, would you be okay with taking me home?"

He shifted closer. "I guess that depends."

"Oh." Her voice sounded breathy. She swallowed. What exactly was happening here? It was like she was on the fringes of reality, like she was an observer as well as a participant. Why deny she'd fantasized about him over the past few days, definitely wondered what being with him would be like if things were even more…intimate between them. Maybe he'd been wondering the same thing… "Depends on what?"

He glanced at her mouth. "Whether you'll let me kiss you again."

Did he mean it or was he just teasing her again? Her scrambled brain came up with the only response she seemed capable of at the moment. "Oh."

He ducked his head, his breathing shallow. Then he closed his eyes briefly, and when he opened them again, intent was stamped onto every feature of his handsome face. He was going to kiss her. Stacey was sure of it.

Her breath caught and she leaned forward, straining toward him in answer to his invitation. Or was she the one casting the invitation? Didn't matter. All that mattered was his next move. This time, *she* dropped her gaze to his mouth.

He lowered his head, and his lips lightly brushed hers. The kiss was soft, tentative almost. So not like the last kiss they'd shared before. She might have been the one to initiate it then, not that she'd known she was kissing him, of course, so it was important to Stacey that he want this enough to be the first to act.

It wasn't long before the kiss turned deeper, more insistent as his tongue teased the seam of her lips apart. *About time.*

Heat spiked through her, drove her down a path that would have an inevitable conclusion. She shivered in anticipation.

Ever since that kiss a few nights ago, she'd been more than curious if the spark between them was just a fluke. That if she *knew* she was kissing Grant, the experience would fall flat. Now, it was impossible to deny that the spark was anything less than a roaring, all-consuming fire. One she was more than happy to walk into.

His hands lightly caressed her, even as they pulled her closer. His heat transferred past the thin barrier of her gown, over her hips, her waist, until she felt his hands on the small of her back.

She trailed her fingers over his chest, his shoulders. He was broad and hard. And, for the moment, hers. All the while his tongue teased, dueled with hers, so much so that she drew him closer, wanting to deepen the kiss, wanting to lose herself with this man, this moment.

Then he tensed before pulling back. What the—

Damn. Someone was behind Grant, not that she'd peer around him to see who it was.

"Yes?" he said, his gaze locked onto Stacey's, and his arms tightened around her. She should've moved away, would've under normal circumstances, but right now, it felt like the safest place for her to be.

"The photographer finally showed up." A woman's voice registered from somewhere behind him. "It's time to do the formal photos for the distillery's brochure."

It took a moment for Stacey's brain to register that the voice belonged to the marketing specialist the distillery owners had hired to direct Grant's public life. Was that regret in his eyes?

She eased in a deep breath. "You'd better go," she told him with a small smile. "I'll get a ride home."

He hesitated, his mouth a tight line before he briefly nodded. "I'll call you later."

The lust fogging her brain began to clear. She shook her head. "Don't. I need to run some errands and plan next week's client dinners. I'll see you at Mom and Dad's tomorrow?"

He raised an eyebrow and squeezed both her hands. "If that's what you want."

No, it wasn't, but it was definitely what needed to happen. She nodded. Because as much as she wanted the kiss to continue, as much as she wanted to see where they'd go together, Stacey knew damn well that Grant had no interest in a real relationship. Ever. And she also knew that starting down a path with him beyond the friendship they had was worse than a dumb idea. It'd be one that could irreversibly wound her.

And she wasn't a glutton for punishment.

# Chapter Seven

Grant stared out the huge kitchen window into the Winters' backyard at what Mrs. Winters had sworn would be a small gathering. By his estimation, she'd invited everyone on the payroll of Winters Construction, the company she and her husband had founded long before the first of their five daughters was born.

He lifted his beer bottle and took a long pull. He was familiar with the Winters family, who was dating whom, who'd broken up with whom, which sister had a crush on another sister's guy. After all, he'd been treated like family since he was eight, and had even worked summers in their construction company so he could help pay for college.

Which made it only natural that he'd be with them on a Sunday afternoon, surrounded by the clan and their closest friends.

What *wasn't* natural was what he'd done with Stacey yesterday.

What the hell had he been thinking? Kissing her was stupid. A mistake. One that wouldn't be repeated if he had a say in it. Trouble was it hadn't changed how damned good it felt to hold her, to pull her close the way he'd imagined doing the past few days. Only an idiot wouldn't like that, and Grant was no idiot.

Or was he?

Damn. He'd not only liked it, he wanted more. Thank God Stacey had come to her senses even though he saw how badly she wanted to give in, knew how badly *he* wanted to give in. Never mind what he'd been thinking—what the hell was he *doing*? Was it worth the risk of losing their friendship? Of losing her completely?

He reached up and massaged the back of his neck. How many times had he asked himself these same questions last night? He'd wanted to text her, but she'd said she'd be busy, which basically meant "leave me alone." And he respected her, was man enough to stop his primal instincts from taking over.

Still, he wasn't any closer to getting answers. He blew out a breath. Maybe he truly was an idiot. Normally, he'd have called Aidan, but his brother was on a late honeymoon, and effectively out of contact for a couple of weeks.

"Penny for your thoughts?"

He turned as Carly plopped onto the kitchen bench beside him. A couple of years older than Stacey, she had the same straight brown hair and easy grin, one that she threw at him as she straightened the collar of his polo shirt. He tilted his beer bottle in her direction. "I hear congratulations are in order for you and Isaac."

She laughed, the sound not quite as rich as Stacey's.

He frowned. Was he going to spend the rest of the afternoon comparing everything to Stacey? He had to fucking get her out of his system or he'd end up with balls too tight to comfortably move.

"There aren't any secrets in this family, are there?" she

groaned.

He stared at her hand. "No ring? I expected you to be sporting some huge rock. You sure Isaac loves you?"

She slapped his upper arm. "Very funny. You know I'm not into that sort of thing. But, yeah, he loves me." She sighed and stared off into the distance. "Just as much as I love him."

"I'll try not to vomit."

She grinned. "Even if you do, it won't change a thing. I'm still marrying the guy."

Anyone with a minimal power of observation could see that Carly and Isaac were meant to be together since they'd had their first formal high-school debate at a regional competition nearly a dozen years ago.

That it had taken them to get through college before they acknowledged each other was no surprise, either. Carly was independent, stubborn, and determined to make her place in the world. On her terms.

And just like Stacey, she accepted help from no one, not even her parents.

He blinked. Shit, he was doing it again. He cleared his throat. "How's the catering biz going?"

"Great." She grinned. "Dinners for Two has really helped me get the word out, so now I'm pretty well booked through summer. Best move I ever made, getting out of law and running my own business." She cocked her head to one side. "So was it Stacey who spilled about the engagement?"

And now they were back to that. To Stacey. "Nope."

"Really." She narrowed her eyes. "She didn't say anything?"

"Don't bother to wait for an answer, because even if she had, I'd never rat her out." Stacey *had* shared that little bit of news as soon as she'd received it. It was a perk of being her best friend. If a guy could actually call it a perk.

At any rate, that's where he needed to firmly stay. In the

friend zone.

"She told me about Leo." Carly shook her head. "What a rat bastard. Good thing you showed up when you did."

"Yeah…" Grant took another swallow of his beer and looked away. Stacey wouldn't have shared all the details of that evening with her sister, would she? He grinned and stared her straight in the eyes. "Good thing, all right."

"Yeah, well…" She shrugged. "All things pay off in time. She just has to wait for Chinaman Hat to work its magic the way it did for me."

He groaned and plunked his bottle on the table. "You don't seriously think burning an offering has anything to do with anything, do you? I thought you had more sense than that."

"Are you saying Stacey's silly?"

"That's different. She's a romantic. She's into white knights and princesses and shit like that." Not that there was anything truly wrong with any of it.

Carly took a swig of her drink but kept her eyes trained on him, a move that Grant was sure she'd perfected in a courtroom. "What about you?" she said after swallowing. "You dating much these days? Or you still chasing the recipe for making the best bourbon around?"

He grunted. Normally a guy didn't talk about stuff like dating with a girl, not that he discussed gory details with anyone except Aidan. But the Winters girls? In the end, Carly was every bit a sister to him. Just the way Stacey was. That is, until he'd kissed her last night.

Who the hell was he kidding? He'd had less than brotherly thoughts about her since *she'd* kissed him awake last weekend. Was it just last weekend? His dick would swear it had been longer than that.

Damn it. He couldn't get the woman out of his brain. And she was definitely both a woman, and on his brain.

"That's your trouble."

He gave Carly a sideways glance. "*What's* my trouble? Or do I really want to know?"

"You don't date enough."

"You have no idea how often I date."

"Maybe not, but I do know it's weird for you to be sitting apart from everyone." She swept an arm out, indicating the large crowd assembled in the backyard.

"How does that even make sense to you?"

"You're acting out of the norm, my friend. Bottom line, I think you need to go out more instead of immersing yourself in yeasts or whatever the hell it is you do to make a batch of bourbon." She waved her hand again. "When all is said and done, coming up with a recipe can't be half as much fun without having someone to share the experience with." She leaned forward. "Right? You know I'm right."

"What're you right about?" Grant looked up as Isaac placed a hand on Carly's shoulder. "Not that I don't think you're right about almost everything."

The mushy words, the mushy looks. This might be how it started for other people, but he knew better than to believe a relationship like theirs was anything he could have. Ever. Not that he wanted anything like that, of course, because he knew how it'd play out. Before long he'd end up attached and thinking a woman loved him unconditionally, only to have her drive off without a look back.

Carly beamed up at her fiancé, complete adoration on her face. "Grant needs to go out more. Know anyone?"

"Actually, yeah." Isaac looked over at him. "She's here, as a matter of fact. Want to meet her?"

He raised an eyebrow. "That's convenient," he said, alternating his gaze between his two friends. "Did you guys plan this?"

She grinned. "Consider it an opportunity."

Why the hell not? This woman might be just the person to erase the memory of kissing Stacey out of his brain.

Grant pasted on what he hoped was an interested smile, then stood. "Let's go."

. . .

Stacey loved her family, really she did. Between her parents, sisters, aunts, uncles, and cousins, get-togethers in her parents' sprawling backyard were always memorable.

There were times, though, when her family tended to be a bit on the overwhelming side. Case in point, her sister Carly's play-by-play of how to bake the perfect lemon flan.

Normally, she'd show some interest in her sister's work, even if only to be polite. Instead, images from yesterday's brunch floated through her brain. A romantic setting, a gorgeous guy, kissing in the moonlight. Well, okay, so there was no moonlight, and while the setting was romantic, she *was* kissing Grant.

And it was perfect.

She'd satisfied her curiosity, all right, so now what? Was it all a big mistake? She drained her glass of strawberry lemonade. Hadn't she read somewhere that life didn't have mistakes? That everything happened for a reason?

*The way burning an offering at Chinaman Hat had ended up with you kind of in bed with Grant?*

Okay, that one *had* to have been a mistake. Or a cruel joke.

*I don't do relationships.*

Grant's frequent claim looped through her head. Kind of like the way she'd drive a couple of loops through a Milestone roundabout whenever she was deep in thought.

Speaking of Grant... She searched through the crowd of family and close friends. For a spring day in central Oregon, they'd lucked out with sunshine and relatively warm temps when their part of the world was just as likely to get snow. She thought for sure he'd be outside, but no. Where had he gone off to? After a brief "hello" when he'd arrived, he'd pretty much disappeared.

Was that on purpose? She did shut him down pretty firmly yesterday. Had she hurt his feelings? Maybe he had regrets about kissing her in the first place? Hell, she wasn't sure *she* had regrets, let alone knew what he thought. There was only one way to find out: go talk to him.

Yeah, it'd be uncomfortable, but didn't one of the relationship blogs state that talking things through was healthy for the relationship? Not that theirs was a *relationship* relationship, but still. And it was best to get it over and done with rather than stew all night. She hoped.

Stacey set her dessert plate down, looked at the chatting circle of women, and caught her sister's gaze across the table.

"Who're you looking for?" Carly asked.

"Grant." Stacey scanned the huge backyard. "Maybe he's inside." Although why he'd choose that was beyond her. The weather really was perfect.

"He's with Meredith."

Meredith?

"God, this chocolate cream pie is da bomb." Carly glanced at Stacey's plate. "You hardly touched it. Don't you like it? I'm trying to pry the recipe from Rose, but she insists that there's a reason Grandma Rose willed it to her for safekeeping." She huffed out a breath. "I don't understand why she'd do that just because Rose was named after her. *I'm* the chef in the family."

Normally Stacey would take the opportunity to tease her sister, but right now there was only one thing on Stacey's brain. She pushed her plate forward.

*Act cool. Act casual. Act like it's no big deal.* "Who's

Meredith?"

"An attorney at Isaac's law firm. He introduced Grant to her, so I suppose they're off somewhere getting to know each other."

Stacey's heart sank and she made herself take slow, deep breaths.

Carly licked her fork before sticking it into the pie on Stacey's plate. "Any idea what's in it that makes it taste so good? Probably something sinfully decadent. Cream or a rich Belgian chocolate or something like that." She blew out a slow breath. "There's got to be a way to get Rose to give up the recipe."

Uh-oh. Carly was coming up with one of her weird ideas. It was the same face she'd made when she'd talked Stacey into accompanying her to Chinaman Hat to burn the offering that eventually netted Isaac. Only this time, Carly's focus was on their older sister. "I'm going to have to blackmail her for it."

"Whatever you decide, leave me out of it." Even as she said the words, Stacey forced herself to stay still. Grant was off with some other woman, getting to know her, and she was happy for him, damn it. He needed to find someone who'd reach through his commitment-phobe exterior and into his soul. Who knew? Maybe this Meredith woman was exactly the one to do that.

And the stab-through-her-heart thing? Well, Stacey would just have to deal. The guy deserved to be happy, so if that meant he found someone new to hang out with, someone he could maybe even fall in love with, that was more than okay with her. It had to be.

The ache in her chest would go away. Eventually.

"You okay?"

She pasted a smile on her face and met her sister's gaze. "Perfectly okay." Because she willed it to be so. Because while Grant wasn't interested in any sort of relationship, he was more than free to pursue any woman *he* found interesting. In much the same way she could pursue any man she found interesting.

*But that kiss...* Both times... Every touch, every nip, was indelibly stamped in her memory. Right along with the sexual tension that snared her from the moment she'd found him in her bed.

She blew out a long breath. Although her head understood the logic, her heart, well, it was having a way harder time.

# Chapter Eight

Chinaman Hat loomed above them, large, majestic, and regal.

While Grant didn't get the whole romantic dinner thing, he *did* recognize a great backdrop when he saw one. Yeah, Julian had something going when he'd insisted that Stacey plan something here.

Which was the whole reason Grant had shown up this afternoon. It was easy to see that she was greatly affected by the old man's terminal cancer diagnosis. While business was important to Stacey, her clients meant far more to her. She was warm and caring and sincere. Always had been.

He pulled a couple of boxes out from the back of her Subaru and turned to find her hunched over a box, her back to him. His brain registered other parts of the scene well. *Very* well. Like the jeans she wore, which were nicely molded to what he knew was a firm ass, one he'd had the privilege of exploring when she'd straddled him the other night. Damn if he'd be able to erase that from his brain anytime soon. Did he even want to?

He tried to tear his gaze away, to admire the scenery.

Something, anything. But she was like a beacon, like a set of flashing lights that had him mesmerized. Besides, shouldn't a guy look in the direction he was going? Otherwise, he'd trip. And if he tripped he could hurt himself, which wouldn't be doing her any favors. So, yeah, it was a safety issue.

She stood abruptly, and he pulled his gaze away. Thinking about his safety was one thing, but getting caught staring? That was an entirely different thing altogether. "Where do you want these?" he asked when he got closer.

She turned with a lantern in each hand and glanced at the boxes he carried. "Careful," she said. "One of those has a container with the fortune cookies from The Chinese Stop. Dennis customized them per Julian's request." She pointed to the small table and sighed. "He's such a romantic."

Yeah, that kind of thing *would* appeal to her. "I suppose that's what the roses are for, too," he said, setting the boxes down.

"Martha's favorite. He's always had roses for her at every dinner I've done for them. Bright red. He said it didn't matter what it cost me to get them." She visibly swallowed and looked away then headed for the worktable discreetly tucked between two sage bushes. "Carly will be here soon."

"What'd she make them?"

"Scallop ceviche, roasted beet salad, and an apricot-stuffed pork tenderloin. She also made her famous truffles for dessert. Another of Martha's favorites."

"Wow. Too bad you don't cook."

"Oh, please." She waved him off. "If you can read a recipe, you can cook anything. It's like another language, that's all. You should try it. Women dig a guy who can cook."

He grunted. "Not my kind of woman."

She stared at him. "That's interesting, but I bet when you find the right woman, you'd gladly learn to cook for her if that's what she wanted."

"Then she'd better like steak a lot."

She looked up and trained her gaze on him, a frown on her face. "Honestly, Grant, I don't understand how you manage to get any woman interested in you at all."

"I have my ways." And once he had their interest, he made sure the woman knew the parameters of the relationship up front: they were going to have fun, and that was all. Dinners, movies, hiking, even. Anything beyond that led to the kind of attachment he refused to let himself have.

If she wanted more than that, he moved on before either of them got hurt.

Stacey set the lanterns down and slid the glass open in one of them. "You really don't have to be here, you know," she said, pulling a candle out and turning it over.

"What if I want to be here?"

The candle's fake flame flickered to life. She lifted her head, her gaze searching his, and it was easy enough to see the question before she posed it. "You're giving up an afternoon where you could be doing something more fun than helping me. How could being here *possibly* be something you'd want to do?"

"I'm here to help out, Stace. I've done that at least a couple of times since you started this business, remember?"

That's exactly why he was here now. For his friend. To be supportive. Nothing more.

*Liar.*

He firmly shoved the mocking accusation to the back of his brain. He was here to help. Period.

"You could be kayaking." She tilted her head, the puzzled look on her face only making her more adorable. "You know, taking one of your new ones out on the river or something."

"I can do that anytime," he insisted. "I've got the afternoon off, so you just go ahead and use me."

There could be a double entendre in there. At least, that's

what his dick was insisting. Damn. All he needed was Stacey to realize he was practically at full mast. "I'm free labor, so might as well," he said quickly, walking past her and toward the parking lot. Better to move while he still could.

He felt awkward. Clumsy. Like he was a teenager again, talking with Milestone High's head cheerleader. Something he'd done because Stacey had first dared him, then told him it was the best way to get over his shyness around girls. She'd convinced him that if he flopped as a teen, he'd have it out of his system so the rest of his life would be pretty great. It'd made sense back then.

Only now he felt like he'd lost more than a decade of progress. He was that tongue-tied teen again. And this time, it was Stacey's presence that made him feel that way. What the *everloving fuck* was wrong with him?

The question rang through his head on a continual loop, from the moment Julian and Martha shuffled from the parking lot, sat through their drinks and appetizers, and then had dinner.

He suspected he knew the answer, and it set off all the warning bells in his head.

So he did what he did best. He buried his emotions.

Grant was there to be supportive through what he knew was a tough time for Stacey. If he had to pound that thought into his brain a thousand times he'd do it. He was *not* going to screw things up by complicating their relationship.

Of course, it'd be tons easier if helping didn't require him needing to be by her side most of the evening. The torture of being around her and not touching her, not kissing her, not pulling her toward him… Deep down, he admitted it was worth it to be around her for a little while. Something about her just made him feel lighter.

And there went the warning bells again.

They worked together quietly, with an ease born of

familiarity. He liked it that way. With one look, one gesture, they moved in sync with each other. One of them poured wine, the other cleared the table. Really, it was no different than the time he'd helped her move into her apartment or when she'd accompanied him to the mayor's brunch. Only this time, he was having one helluva hard time not thinking of all the not-just-friends things he'd love to do with her.

"Son, how about giving my lady a hand up, would you?"

Julian's request snapped Grant out of his thoughts, and he straightened from where he'd been leaning against a tree trunk.

"I can do it," Stacey offered. She set down the carafe of water on the staging table.

"Let Grant do it." He smiled, planted his cane in the dirt, and rose to his feet. "Maybe I'd like to have a word with him."

The old man wanted to talk? This should be interesting. "I hope you don't want relationship advice, 'cause I'm not your guy."

"He isn't kidding, Julian." Stacey grabbed up the napkins. "He's got commitment issues."

"At least I don't believe in white knights and princesses."

She propped a hand on her hip. "I don't know why you bother to deny the existence of either."

"Dreamer."

"And not apologizing for it one bit." She headed toward the plastic bins she'd stashed away.

Julian chuckled. "Now, kids, no need to argue." He turned until he faced Grant. "Believe me, son, it isn't worth arguing. She's going to get her way whether you think she should or not."

"That's good to know." Grant took the bouquet of roses off the table, then offered his arm and held himself steady as Martha grasped onto it. She sure had a firm grip for someone so small.

"Thank you, young man," she said, tentatively rising to her feet. "You're nice and strong."

Julian chuckled from behind him. "Just remember who you're sleeping with tonight."

"Oh, Jules, you know there isn't another man out there for me." She winked at Grant. "Doesn't matter how handsome he might be." Her voice was as light and playful as her husband's. "Of course, some men's looks do improve with age."

"I would hope so." Julian took her hand, raising it to his lips.

Grant shifted uncomfortably from one foot to the other. Did he just stumble into a private moment or what? Talk about awkward.

Now what should he do? He couldn't exactly step back and let them have their privacy. Not with the way Martha was clinging to his arm.

He pulled his gaze away from the couple. There was no denying that whatever these two had going seemed to work.

Martha patted her husband's arm. "We should get going. Pearl's not gonna stand around all night." She pointed to the woman by the waiting car in the parking lot.

Grant squinted at the tiny older woman beside the silver Cadillac. "Is she all right to drive?"

"Pearl? Oh, sure," Julian answered. "She's got a pillow on the seat so she can see over the steering wheel."

Yeah... Maybe he should offer to drive all three of them home and grab a taxi back.

"Pearl's chauffeured us around the past couple of years. She's fine."

"Ummm...okay."

Grant looked from one to the other as the three of them slowly inched along the gravel path. He tried to think of something to say. "How long have you two been married? If you don't mind my asking?" Didn't old people like answering questions like that?

"You tell him, Jules. Unless you don't remember," Martha said with a mock sniff.

"You kidding me, woman? Is this some sort of test? Because you know I'll remember that day forever." Julian stopped and regarded Grant with sharp eyes. "Sixty years, son. And if you're lucky, you'll get to experience the same thing with a woman of your own."

That's right. He vaguely remembered Stacey mentioning this. "You never know," he lied.

But he *did* know. Maybe others were willing to expose themselves to vulnerability, but Grant knew better. Even if it paid off for other people, he was different. People always left him. Look at his mom. Look at the half a dozen foster families who'd sent him on his way. Sure, he was fun when he was a still a kid, but in the end, he wasn't someone any of them had wanted to keep.

Really. If his own mother couldn't be bothered to keep him, why would anyone?

No way was he opening himself up to that kind of pain.

"Now, Jules, don't make assumptions. Maybe Grant prefers men."

Prefers men? Holy fuck. He didn't give off that vibe, did he? "Uh, no, actually. I prefer women."

"Oh, good," Martha said. "Because it's easy to see that you and Stacey like each other. A lot."

"Sure we do. We're best friends."

"That's all?" Julian asked.

They stopped again, and the older couple stared at him.

"That's all." Grant said the words firmly. Because that's the way it needed to be.

"That's interesting. I'm rarely wrong about these things." Julian shrugged as they resumed their trek toward the parking lot.

"Julian's predicted which of our friends would have successful relationships," Martha added. "Of course, some of them didn't listen when he'd told them *not* to get too involved with someone." She sighed. "He's a good matchmaker. Look at us."

They stopped again as Julian leaned in toward Martha, planting a quick kiss on her lips.

The older woman giggled. "Oh, Jules, stop. What will people think?"

If anyone had told Grant he'd be involved in a conversation between two old folks about marriage, he'd have made a bet and obviously lost. Might as well ask the burning question on his brain. "What's the secret to staying married so long?"

"The secret to staying married? Why, that's easy." The old man carefully placed the tip of his cane to one side of a rock. "A guy's gotta know that the woman he marries is his other half, nothing less than that. Because when you treat her like she's a part of who you are, there's no way you wouldn't do what's best for the relationship."

Huh. That made some sense.

"And," Martha said, "It isn't enough to love each other. You gotta be sure to touch a lot, too." She winked at Julian this time.

Geez. Now the two old people were flirting with each other. Grant wasn't sure if he should be honored or amused or what. He chose the middle ground. Always safer that way. "Right. Good to know."

"In my experience, when you do find that special woman, life takes on a whole new meaning," the man continued. "Everything tastes better and sounds better. You smile when you wake up in the morning, and you can't wait to see each other at the end of the day. Love's powerful stuff, son. Powerful stuff."

All Grant could do was stare, helpless.

Julian chuckled. "Don't you worry too much, son," he said once they reached the waiting car and the driver who appeared to be as old as they were. "You treat Stacey right, and she'll be by your side your entire life."

Stacey?

"Uh…Stacey? Wait… We're not…"

"Oh, I know," the man said, waving him off with one hand. "You're best friends. Believe me, I know." He smiled at his wife. "That's how we started."

Grant tensed. It was just because Martha was hanging onto his arm for dear life while she got into the back of the sedan. That was all. It had nothing to do with the image the man had planted in Grant's brain.

Julian had hobbled to the other side of the car by the time Grant had Martha seated, the bouquet of roses safely in her lap. Once the couple was securely belted in, the old man leaned toward him. "You remember what I said, young man, and do right by Stacey. You do that and I promise you, the love you get in return will be worth it. You hear?"

Arguing with a dying octogenarian seemed like a dick move, so Grant just nodded, then closed the door and stepped back as the sedan slowly edged forward.

He wouldn't find himself involved in a more-than-friends relationship with Stacey. Ever. He was a live-in-the-moment kind of guy who rolled with what life shot his way. And while the whole kissing thing and the practically-naked-straddling-him thing had happened with her, it didn't mean he had to live there. He'd move on, see what was around the next turn in life's road.

Because that's who he was.

# Chapter Nine

Stacey had known Grant for years, knew everything there was to know about him. She'd watched him experience all the hurt and confusion and *loneliness* an eight-year-old could feel.

She knew about his battle with shyness, knew how painful it was for him to stand on the perimeter of any crowd when he wanted so badly to be included. She also knew his resilience, saw his confidence deepen, saw his unconditional loyalty and devotion to the people in his life, despite his tomorrow-be-damned attitude.

But the way he'd gently guided Martha and Julian to their waiting car? Well, that carved an even deeper groove in Stacey's heart. It was almost like she was seeing him for the first time, and her heart definitely approved of what was there.

She pulled off her hair band and redid her ponytail. What, exactly, did she feel for Grant? She snapped the band in place. The whole thing was so damned confusing, but no matter what she felt for her best friend, he'd made it clear he wasn't interested in any kind of a long-term, romantic relationship.

Every relationship webinar she'd attended instructed women to believe a guy when he said such things, thus challenging them to leave him and find someone else. Easy to say when feelings weren't involved.

She blew out a breath and placed the wineglasses in a bin. Oh, sure, she could deny every ounce of what she was feeling for him, and might even convince herself the denial was truth, but she knew better. So now the question was, what the hell was she going to do about it?

She pulled a slipcover off a chair. The attraction wasn't one-sided. Grant was just as affected. She saw it in the look in his eyes and the way she'd caught him staring at her, felt it each time he'd held onto her hand longer than normal, or even in the way he'd text to say good night. Not that he hadn't done those things before, but while Stacey couldn't quite put a finger on it, things were…different.

"How about some help?"

A thrill shot through her at the sound of his voice. *Oh, for Pete's sake.* She forced back the shock of desire that traced through her, and concentrated on folding the chair closed instead.

"I've got this," she said, glancing at him and nodding toward the table. "How about folding that up?"

He silently maneuvered the table onto its edge, and all the while every part of her hummed to life, drawn to the way he effortlessly did as she'd asked. There was definitely something attractive about a strong, capable man, whether he was folding up a table or taking care of the mundane things necessary to get through life.

She openly watched him haul the table toward her SUV. His muscles rippled underneath his form-fitted T-shirt, and while she wasn't sure why he didn't appear affected by the dropping temperatures, she didn't really care.

She dug her fingernails into her palms to keep herself grounded.

It was hard not to stare when he started back across the paved path that separated the parking lot from the grassy area. This was Grant. Who he was. How he'd always dressed. No pretense, no airs. Just Grant.

And she'd only just noticed him. Like *really* noticed him.

But while a part of her might secretly want him, Grant Phillips would never be hers.

The knowledge brought a longing to her chest, one that reached inside and dragged her soul forward. To find someone to be beside her, believe in her dreams…why was that so impossible? Was it really too much to ask of life? She didn't want a bunch of men, just one. *The* one.

Her senses went on hyperalert the moment Grant returned. "Julian and Martha," he said, shaking his head with a smile on his face. "What a couple."

"They're great, aren't they?"

"I can see why Julian's your favorite client," he said, taking a lantern off a shepherd's hook and handing it over to her. "You deal with the candle, okay?"

"Can't figure out how to turn it off?" she teased.

"More like I'm afraid I'll break it," he said drily.

"What did you talk about?" She reached for the other lantern and kept her hands occupied. It was either that or run the risk of hauling herself into his arms.

"What makes you think we talked about much?"

"*Pfft*. Are you kidding me? I've known Julian for way longer than you have. He's great at passing on his wisdom, so there was a pretty good chance you got a dose of it."

"Oh, I did all right." He turned to her, then, the look on his face a mixture of curiosity and… She sucked in a deep breath. His blue eyes were wide, his pupils dilated.

*Whoa.*

"He said that if I treated you right, you'd be beside me for as long as I lived."

Stacey blinked, the words registering and the heat creeping up her face. "He didn't say that."

Grant only stared at her. "He did."

She gulped. It most certainly *sounded* like something the older man would say. And Julian didn't bother to share his thoughts with those he figured weren't up to hearing his take on life, which pretty much meant that he believed that Grant was okay.

It wasn't anything new to her, of course, but was it another reason, possibly, maybe, to think that these feelings she had for Grant might possibly, *maybe* lead to something between them?

Stacey gave herself a mental shake. What the hell did any of that even mean? Did it even make sense? Thank God he wasn't privy to any of her thoughts, as jumbled as they'd been the past few days.

She cleared her throat. "I guess that's Julian for you."

They loaded up the last of the supplies she'd brought, and when she was sure they'd left nothing behind, she turned to him. "Thanks for being here tonight. I…uh…that is…"

She gave herself another mental shake. What was wrong with her? She heaved in a deep breath, and her gaze locked with his. A soft, steady hum started deep in her belly, touching a chord that made her inhale sharply. "I really appreciate it."

He stepped toward her. "You okay?"

"Yeah. Just…" She tried to pull her gaze from his, but something there tethered her to him.

"Don't do that, Stace."

"Do what?"

"Look at me like that."

She licked her lips, and his gaze dropped down to her

mouth.

He swallowed. "When you look at me like that, I think things I shouldn't."

His honesty was expected, but there was that hint of vulnerability she'd rarely seen in him over the years, one she knew he shielded from the world. That he would reveal it now...

Her heartbeat stopped on the edge of hyperdrive. This was her chance to throw herself off the cliff, to glide on the wind and soar. She strangled the logic that insisted she couldn't defy gravity and would crash to Earth instead.

"How am I looking at you?" Her voice was breathless, one she barely recognized.

He grinned, and with Chinaman Hat behind him, he looked breathtakingly gorgeous. "Like you want to take part in my less-than-friendly thoughts."

"In an action flick sort of way, or more of a rom-com type?"

He raised an eyebrow. "You sure you really want to know?"

His voice was low, quiet, his gaze trained on hers with an intensity that sent a shiver chasing down her spine.

"Well?" he prompted.

"Oh...well...I..." Stacey blinked, then pulled her gaze to a spot over his shoulder before landing on his again. What was she supposed to say to that?

Grant shoved a hand through his hair and glanced away. "Look, Stace. I don't want things to be weird between us."

She could turn on an air of bravado, could pretend to misunderstand, or she could finally gather the courage to move the relationship forward.

She was still contemplating her options when he reached out a hand. He caressed her face before tilting her chin up until their gazes locked. "We don't need to rock the boat or anything. Okay?"

*What if I want to?*

She wasn't sure she *totally* wanted to go there, but it was enough to know that he felt something, too. "Okay," she said, warmth spreading through her with that knowledge, burning a blaze from where skin touched skin. How she'd never experienced this before with Grant, or anyone else, for that matter, seemed impossible to her, and yet, there it was.

"Good." He dropped his hand and his gaze briefly searched hers. "Let's get this stuff dropped off at Carly's, then I'll make sure you get home okay."

She forced in a breath to clear her brain. That's right, they had to go by her sister's house, where Carly had converted her garage into an industrial kitchen, and where she kept a small storage space for Stacey. "You don't have to do that."

"Maybe I want to."

Her brain told her he was just being a good friend, but her heart was practically doing cartwheels in her chest. "Grant?"

"Yeah?"

Through a hammering heart she swallowed down the case of nerves that'd opened up, then she briefly contemplated backing out. No, she had to plunge forward if she wanted to see where the relationship could go. "What if I told you I don't think I want to be alone tonight?"

"In an action flick sort of way or more the rom-com type?"

He threw her words back at her, his gaze dropping to her mouth before flickering up to capture her eyes again. He oozed testosterone, looked like he could barely control it, too, judging by the way he held himself like he was ready to pounce.

She mentally fanned herself. Good God, she wasn't sure she could handle the sexual energy.

She should make a smart-ass joke out of the whole thing,

do whatever it would take to drop the tension that filled the air around them, surrounding them like the clouds that circled the top of Chinaman Hat. At least, that was what a smart woman would do. But, apparently, she was missing a few brain cells at the moment.

He reached out and traced the outline of her jaw, the smile on his face mirroring the desire in his eyes. "Let's take this to Carly's, then we can head over to your place. Whatever you decide from there is fine with me, okay?"

He was leaving it up to her. So like him to take everything in stride no matter how good—or awful—it was.

*Deep breath. Take a deep breath.*

She willed her body to do what her brain commanded. After all, it wasn't like he'd never been to her place after one of her events. Just the two of them hanging out on her bed watching a Netflix movie on her laptop. Although there was a pretty sure bet that Netflix in bed wasn't going to happen tonight.

The next half hour was a blur, and by the time they'd reached her apartment she was a tangled mass of nerves again. To feel nervous around him was so foreign, she half wondered if the experience would be worth it.

He stepped into the apartment, the door closing decisively shut. Stacey turned. He leaned with his back against it, all casual, all male, and, if she was brave enough, all hers.

A corner of his mouth tipped up. "Half an hour until the pizza shows up. What do we do until then?"

# Chapter Ten

Stacey's heart was going to gallop out of her chest, she was sure of it.

"Ummm..." She looked around. "What do you mean?"

She was stalling. Why was she stalling? And why couldn't she breathe?

"I think you know exactly what I mean." He pushed away from the door and closed the distance between them, stopping a foot away. Far enough to give her space, yet close enough she could feel the heat emanating from him. "Unless you don't want this, which is totally okay. You know that, right?"

When she didn't answer—*couldn't* answer—he stepped back and shoved a hand through his hair, momentarily disturbing the loose curls there. "Okay. How about a movie? Out here," he quickly added. "Maybe you could bring the laptop out and we'll set it up on the coffee table."

"I'll go get it." She practically ran to her bedroom, needing a second to get her head on straight. She'd wanted this, right? He was clearly open to the possibility. What was *wrong* with her?

The tension between them had eased by the time she returned to the living room. "Who's turn to pick?"

"Mine."

"Ugh." She placed her laptop on the coffee table and sagged on the sofa. "I'm not in the mood for an action flick."

"And I'm not in the mood for a rom-com." He plugged the laptop into an outlet across the room. "How about we random scroll?"

Random scroll. It'd been at least a couple of months since they'd disagreed on a movie to the point where they'd pulled up Netflix and chosen one by closing their eyes and randomly moving the cursor. Wherever it stopped, that was what they watched. "Are you sure? We could end up with something pretty bad."

"Or pretty good." He shrugged. "We've discovered a few decent movies that way."

"Good point." She blew out a breath. What she needed tonight was a distraction. Who really cared if it was something she could get into or not? And even if she couldn't, they'd established this system years ago, and it'd eliminated conflict since. "Okay, you put your finger on the screen, and I'll scroll."

When Grant was in position, they both closed their eyes. "One, two, three," she said slowly, then randomly flicked the computer's mouse.

"Stop," Grant said.

She opened her eyes. "*The Big Easy*." She frowned. "It looks old. Have you seen it?"

"No." He plopped down on the sofa next to her.

She scrolled through the description. "Great. A drama." This just wasn't going to be her night, was it?

"You know the rules. We have to watch at least the first half hour before we can nix it for something else."

"Who made up that dumb rule, anyway?"

"You did." He glanced at his phone. "We've got about twenty-five minutes before the pizza arrives, assuming it gets here on time. If we decide to watch something else we can do it then."

"It better get here on time," she grumbled.

Stacey started the movie and leaned back, realizing too late that she and Grant were practically touching.

So what? It's not like she hadn't ever sat with her head turned into his shoulder while watching a particularly gruesome part of a movie.

The story started out interestingly enough, if you considered a murder interesting, anyway. Subtitles played along the bottom of the screen, a necessary evil since they were just as likely to talk as to watch.

"Hey, thanks again for all the help today," she said. "It made the time go quicker."

"No problem. I already told you I didn't mind."

"I just don't want you to think I'm taking advantage of you, that's all."

"I don't feel that way. How's it possible that Julian's so ill?" Grant asked after a brief pause. "He doesn't look it."

"He says his attitude is a choice he makes every day. He figures that he's only got so much time left, and he didn't want to spend it hurting himself as well as the only woman he'd ever loved." She sighed. "It's one of the most romantic things I've ever heard."

"How *that* romantic?"

She twisted around to gape at him. "Are you kidding? No matter how awful he feels he's choosing to live his life the best way he knows how. Not just for himself, but for Martha, the love of his life. That's romantic."

He just shrugged.

How could some guys totally get that while others, like Grant, remained clueless?

She settled back into her spot, and they watched the movie in companionable silence, as the female lead—an assistant DA—grilled the cop she was working with.

"Dennis Quaid was really hot even back then," Stacey murmured.

"I suppose. I have a thing for the Anne character, myself."

"Well, good. I'd be a bit worried if you had a thing for Dennis Quaid."

Grant angled himself so he was turned in her direction, and while she couldn't see him, she felt him, felt the weight of his stare.

"What?"

He shrugged again.

"Look, either say what's on your brain or watch the movie, but don't just stare. It's unnerving."

"Okay, tell me something. Julian and Martha have been married for sixty years. Do you really think they got along *every second* of that time?"

That was on his brain? Now? "I thought you didn't believe in relationships."

"I'm being serious."

She sighed. "Maybe not every second, but on the whole the good times clearly outweighed the bad. There are plenty of people in great, long-lasting relationships. Not perfect or anything, but seems to me that the love they share with their partner makes it easier to deal with the tough times. Maybe that's what adds to the bliss."

He went quiet and it took everything Stacey had not to look at him.

"Well," he finally said. "That sounds like something a girl would think up."

In other words, he still didn't believe it was possible. At least not for him.

"Hey, you asked for my opinion, and that's what you got."

She kept her eyes on the screen and her voice as normal as possible. "Why? Are you thinking you might be open to a relationship one of these days?"

She was pretty sure he couldn't hear her pounding heart, but she didn't dare look at him. Probably safer to watch the movie, where the main characters were at some restaurant.

"Me?" He shook his head. "Hell, no. I was just wondering if there's a new angle we can take at the brewery. You know, something to draw in the older crowd. Celebrations and such."

"Liar."

"Why would you say that?"

She laughed. "I've known you forever. You only ask questions like that when you're curious enough to entertain an idea."

"I ask questions to gather information," he grumbled. "Then I get to reserve judgment on my thoughts about a topic."

"Which in this case is about relationships."

He stared. She could feel it.

Stacey grinned. "So, you have to at least admit you're curious if relationships have staying power."

"I'm just saying, how much sense does it make to plan for a future that might never come? There are no guarantees."

Groaning, Stacey tucked her foot under her knee and faced him. "Because there aren't guarantees about anything. Life should be *balanced*. Does it make sense to spend all your energy on the now without thinking about the future? Nothing about now is guaranteed, either, you know."

He grinned at her.

"What's so funny?"

He raised his arms above his head in a stretch that left very little to the imagination when his shirt crept above the top of his jeans and showed off the trail that wandered down to Happy Land.

Oh, wow. She swallowed.

"Do you have this kind of discussion with all the guys you date?"

It was a deflection, but a good one. "Do you?"

"I don't date guys," he answered smoothly. "But you really ought to know that this type of conversation is too heavy for most guys to wrap their heads around. You're probably scaring them off."

Never mind that *he* started it. She sighed. "I need a guy who can keep up with me. Is that such a bad thing?"

"Do you want a guy or a racehorse?"

"How about a guy who's hung like a horse? Who's got more than a few brain cells and knows how to laugh, too?"

"Sounds like a challenge."

"You have no idea." She shifted back and tried to follow the movie instead of the line of thinking that would lead her straight into imagining just how well-endowed Grant would be. *Gulp.* "Are we watching this or what?"

They settled back in, but she could barely concentrate, could barely follow along given her proximity to Grant, to the fact that the only reason they were sitting on the couch was because they couldn't set foot in her bedroom without things getting…intimate.

"You cold?" Grant leaned over and brushed strands of hair from where they'd fallen across her face, then bumped his shoulder against hers. "I could grab a blanket if you like."

And he would, too. That was the way he'd been for years, that's what made him so comfortable to be around, that's what made him such a good, reliable friend. Only, tonight he didn't feel like just a friend. He felt like more. So much more.

"I'm fine." She smiled up at him. "I was just thinking that it feels good to have you here." Yeah, it did. It felt good. It felt *right*. But she could think of something that'd feel even better.

"Funny. I was thinking the same thing."

"You were?"

"Yeah." He reached for her hand and locked their fingers, rubbing his thumb over the back of her hand in an absentminded fashion.

Still, there was something about the way he did it, with his gaze glued to her laptop like he was completely fascinated by the story playing out on it, even though a part of her suspected he wasn't seeing a thing. Was she wrong about all this?

On the screen the main characters argued...and then Remy, the Dennis Quaid character, planted himself in front of Anne, effectively trapping her to the chair she sat in. Tension crackled in the air around them, and he leaned forward, his face inches from hers.

Desire and passion registered, and Stacey held her breath, the scene so sensual she couldn't help herself. Remy closed the remaining few inches between them, capturing Anne in a kiss so intense that Stacey shivered, because the characters weren't just kissing, but *kissing*.

"Did I miss something?" Grant asked beside her. "I thought this was a pseudo-thriller movie."

"It is." It just apparently had some very hot, very sexy bits in it, too. Bonus.

Remy and Anne were now in bed, and Stacey's fuck-me meter shot up, every cell in her body on hyperalert. They knelt and kissed and touched, skin against skin, mouths meeting, then pulling away as Remy made his way down Anne's neck to her shoulder, probably not caring that her clothes were in the way, from the looks of things.

Beside her Grant remained silent, but the pressure on her hand increased, the circles he drew with his thumb were more intense, the feeling erotic and sending traces of awareness skipping up her arm. It probably helped that she sat so close to him—she was practically in his lap. She fought the need to squirm, to assuage that perfect spot between her legs that throbbed with need.

She looked away from the screen and bit down on her lower lip. Damn, damn, damn. She was tired of waiting for the perfect guy to show up. Grant was here, and he would willingly give her what she wanted tonight. Why was she fighting it so hard? Maybe he was right after all. Would it be so bad to focus on *now*, without thought of what a future might look like?

She couldn't stand it. His hand stroking hers, the warmth of his body pressed next to her, the thump of her heart like it wanted to gallop out of her chest. What was so wrong with taking what she wanted, damn it?

Not a thing. Not. A. Damn. Thing.

Without a word she shifted, untangling their hands, hoping he understood her silent intent. She leaned toward Grant, acutely aware that something very interesting was happening on the screen. Didn't matter, she had more pressing matters in front of her.

She traced a hand over his chest, felt the rock-hard muscles underneath, and sighed. Sure, she'd seen him with his shirt off before, but chances were good that they weren't half as appealing then as they would be now that she'd let her mind go down that path.

Stacey pulled back just far enough to capture his gaze. His breathing was shallow, his eyes trained on her like he had no intention of breaking their connection. "You know what we should do, Grant?"

"What?"

She smiled at the breathlessly spoken word. He was definitely as turned on as she was. What would he think if she suggested they mimic the scene playing out on the screen? "I

think we should—"
*Ding-dong!*

...

Grant blinked as the sound of the doorbell registered and Stacey scrambled off the sofa. *Holy motherfucking God.*

A few seconds earlier and he'd have already hauled her to her bedroom, missing the doorbell completely. Grant wouldn't have stopped. Screw the pizza.

"Get the door," she directed, fumbling for her purse. Her hands were shaking, and she looked as flustered as she sounded.

Easy for her to say. She didn't have a woody that made walking hard. Somehow, he managed to make it to the door, but not before the doorbell rang again. He threw open the door and glared at the guy standing there, totally unaware that he'd just cock-blocked Grant.

"I've got a Bear Lakes pizza," the guy said, holding out the box.

Grant grabbed it while Stacey shoved some bills out. "Here. Keep the change."

With the door firmly closed behind them, she led the way to the kitchen. "Wow. Smells good. I hope they remembered to leave off the mushrooms. I never did like those on my pizza. I don't think most places know how to cook them right. Either that or they use canned mushrooms. I don't like canned mushrooms."

She was babbling, stringing words together, filling the silence with anything that would distract herself from facing what was in front of her. He'd seen it all before.

"Go ahead and set that down, and I'll get the plates."

To hell with this.

She opened a cabinet, and he quickly slammed it shut and

held it in place. The face she turned to him held a mixture of confusion and something else, something unidentifiable, yet sparked an answering response inside him. She was sweetness and passion and desire all melded together into one amazing woman.

He was acting on instinct, he knew, and he also knew that he could be wrong. But, damn it, they'd been dancing around this "thing" between them long enough.

"Grant?"

Her confusion was his advantage. He pulled Stacey close, saw the moment her confusion morphed into desire.

"If you don't want this, tell me now." His voice was gruff, demanding, driven by a need so intense he wasn't sure he could contain it.

A soft smile curved her lips, the perfect contrast to the hard edge of his control. Stacey pulled his head down to hers and rose onto her toes.

*Finally...*

He relished her soft sighs and moans, and nibbled his way down the side of her neck. Her moans grew louder when he reached a particularly sensitive spot. Hmm. He needed to catalog the location for future reference.

He wasn't sure when it happened or how it happened, but at some point, it registered that he had her pinned up against the refrigerator, her kisses now deeper, more insistent, more demanding. And, God help him, he was more than happy to give in to her wishes, her desires.

Because tonight would be all about her.

# Chapter Eleven

The refrigerator. She was pinned between Grant's hard body and the smooth front of the refrigerator. Excitement raced through her as his mouth plundered, retreated, then plundered again. It was an assault on her senses like no other, a sweet devotion and a demanding master all at the same time. And Stacey loved every second of it.

She moaned and tightened her arms around his neck, shifted her hips, then wrapped a leg around one of his. All the while his kisses engulfed her, creating a haze so sweet that the spot between her legs throbbed. Slowly, she ground herself against him, sensations ripping through her with each move up and down, up and down, craving the friction, craving the intensity, wanting more.

Dear God, she couldn't remember the last time she'd been this turned on. She just wanted to feel, to savor this moment.

"You enjoying yourself there, baby doll? I promise there're even better ways of making you feel good."

The whispered words brushed against her like a caress,

and the pressure between her legs increased, making her move her hips even more. "Yeah? What did you— *Oh...*"

Cupping her bottom, he raised her off the floor and she wrapped her legs around his waist. He pressed her hard against him, creating a sensation so erotic that she threw her head back, her moans edging higher.

He chuckled, then pressed harder against her. "Yeah. I'm guessing you like this, huh?" Then the kisses started again before she could decipher his words, let alone answer. This time he began on the side of her neck, pleasure tripping through her from the contact of his rough beard. Her nipples tightened and the hard bud between her legs throbbed.

Stacey gasped and ground herself against his thick ridge. "Well, what do we have here?" He was hard. Incredibly large.

"If you don't know, I'm not sure I should be the one to tell you."

He licked the sensitive spot on the side of her neck, sending a tide of electrical pulses through her. The tingles multiplied into a thousand points of light coursing through every part of her, making her hypersensitive, leaving her wanting.

"Grant." She angled her neck, silently inviting him to continue to explore, to learn her body, learn what she liked, in the same way she intended to learn his.

He groaned. "I'm so fucking turned on."

His words torched a path through her, so much so that she wanted to do as much for him as he was doing for her. *This* she liked. This she could do. It was a rush of feminine power, a heady sensation of knowing she was in control and didn't have plans to stop anytime soon.

"You're killing me here," he whispered, his hips connecting with hers in a slow, sensual grind.

She nipped at the side of his neck and was rewarded with another groan. Her skin tingled, each nerve ending prickling with intensity, wanting more, ready for more. He was so strong, yet so gentle, holding her against him like she was the most precious thing in the world. Like she was cherished.

Movement registered a split second later, and she tightened her legs around his waist. "Where are we going?"

"Bedroom."

"Too far away." She wanted him here, now.

"Uh-uh. I'm taking you where I know you'll be comfortable."

Another round of warmth enveloped her. "You're incredible, you know."

He chuckled. "And I haven't even started yet."

They crossed the doorway and toward her bed. Thank God she'd forgotten to turn off the lamp when she grabbed the laptop. The last thing she wanted to do was poke a sensitive spot because the blackout curtains were drawn.

His eyes turned serious as he knelt on her bed and laid her down. Then his hands got busy. Super busy. He ran his fingers down her sides, slowly, erotically, until he reached the hem of her T-shirt. "This is your last chance to back out, Stace."

He'd do it, too, even though she could see the effort it would cost him. "I thought we crossed that bridge a while ago." Her gaze locked with his and she reached a hand to his face. "Don't you *dare* stop."

"Not a chance." He tugged the shirt over her head but stopped short of removing it completely. His eyes narrowed slightly and his breathing shallowed.

Ever since *that night*, Stacey had caved to her desire to wear the prettiest bra and panty sets she owned. They made her feel feminine and sexy, even underneath a T-shirt and jeans. Tonight was no exception. Thank God. The pink demi-bra pushed her breasts up and made them seem bigger, fuller, making it one of her favorites.

"Beautiful." His voice was tinged with awe.

The word fueled the pleasure already unleashed inside her. It was honest, romantic even. Then he reached a hand out to cup first one breast then the other, and she sat up farther, bit down on her bottom lip and pushed into him. He skimmed a thumb over a nipple, and underneath the sheer lace, it puckered. She gasped, leaned back, and closed her eyes, sensuality washing over her while his mouth and hands skimmed over her body.

The electric pulses were in full force, tingling through her with each pass of his hands, each lick on her breasts, her neck, her lips. And all she could do was lie back and take it in, enjoy the exquisite sensations of her body humming to life. She squirmed, wanting the release, aching for what she knew would eventually be hers.

Wordlessly, Grant leaned over and nuzzled the space between her breasts, then turned to one side, licking his way toward the point and capturing the lace-covered tip in his mouth.

"Oh, God."

He chuckled. "You like that."

"Don't you?" she gasped.

"More than you know." As if to prove it, he lowered his head once more, this time teasing his way through the valley between her breasts, not quite touching each peak.

She groaned and wriggled her hands, still effectively trapped in her shirt. "Not fair." She gasped the words out, her body giving in to the moment, to the spell that seemed to have been cast around them.

He licked and sucked, alternating pressure, keeping her off-balanced.

"Grant."

He seemed intent on ignoring her, his mouth working its magic against her sensitized skin.

"Grant, please," she gasped again.

"Please what?" he asked, pulling away and undoing the front clasp on her bra. He gazed into her eyes. "Maybe this is how I like you."

She tilted her head and caught a glimpse of her shirt, his hand effectively holding it in place. "With my hands above my head so you have to do all the work?"

"I promise this isn't work. This is play."

"Maybe I wanna play, too."

"You'll get your chance. But, me first." Still, he released his hold on her hands and pulled the shirt completely off.

Stacey didn't waste time sitting up and shrugging off her bra before tugging at the hem of his T-shirt. "I think this has to go."

"You got something against ZZ Top?" he asked. "This is one of my favorite shirts."

"I know that, but right now, it's covering up something I've wanted to get a good look at for days now. Mmmm… nice," she said, once the shirt was off. She splayed her hands over his chest, relished the light dusting of hair. "But I want to see more."

He responded to the slight push she gave him, turning and shifting until he was on his back. She scrambled to her knees, trailed her fingers over his chest and toward the top of his jeans.

Her heart hammered. She wanted this, wanted him. Once she undid the button, she leaned forward, planting a kiss at the band as she slowly dragged the zipper down.

Pulling back, she stared at the strain against his underwear. "Looks like you're ready to play."

"Maybe you should take a closer look. You know, just to be sure."

She grinned. "Good point."

Off came the jeans and boxer briefs, and it was all Stacey

could do to contain herself. Magnificent. Impressive. Hers.

She lowered her head and lightly brushed her mouth against his thick erection, then blew a stream of warm air over him. He was all musky male, the tip of his cock with its drop of pre-cum beckoning her closer.

She positioned herself between his legs and rubbed her hands over the sensitive flesh on either side of his straining cock. Glancing up, she caught his gaze, lowered her head, and swirled her tongue around him.

He moaned, the sound fueling her own moans of appreciation, but it wasn't long before he clasped her face with both hands, effectively stilling her. "Stacey." Her name seemed torn from him. "Stop or I'm going to lose it."

She licked her lips. "We wouldn't want that."

"No, we wouldn't." He sat up and gazed into her eyes, the simple connection instilling a deeper, stronger sense of trust. But it'd always been this way with Grant, hadn't it? She trusted him more than she'd trusted anyone else in her life.

He kissed her, then, his touch so erotic on her sensitive skin while he laid her back and worked his way down her oh-so-willing body. She closed her eyes, reveling in the contact, anticipating more. She was so attuned to the hum of her body, to the way he skillfully played his hands over her, to how he had her fully undressed before the thought even registered.

It didn't take long for him to be between her legs, thank God, but he didn't exactly dive in right away, either. Instead he ran light circles on the insides of her thighs, then lowered his head.

Stacey held her breath, the seconds drifting by into what she was sure was a full-on minute. "Grant." Yeah, there was desperation in her voice, and she reached for his head, wanting so badly to pull him into position.

"Yeah?"

"Grant, please." She was panting, her breaths coming

hard and fast.

"Please what?"

She raised her hips, anticipation building. He blew a warm breath over her core, then nuzzled her, teased her so that when he finally flicked his tongue over her, she arched off the bed, sure she'd combust into a heap of want, of need. "God, yes," she moaned, her hands automatically reaching out to hold his head in place.

The insistent pressure of his mouth, of his fingers working in rhythm with each pass of his tongue… The combination had her pressing her heels into the mattress as the tension built inside. God, he was good, taking her right to the brink as if he knew how badly she needed the release. And then it finally ripped through her in a powerful rush, pulses of light flashing behind her closed eyes.

When the world slowed, he pushed himself off of her.

"Grant?"

"Condom." His gaze was desperate. "Please tell me you have some."

"In the bathroom, second drawer down."

Fortunately, it wasn't long before he was back.

She raised up on one elbow and grinned. "The whole box? Kind of ambitious, aren't you?"

He pulled out a packet and ripped it open. "I like being prepared." He rolled the condom on and positioned himself over her, then stroked her face with the back of his hand, his touch so gentle that her heart ached. "I think this was where we left off."

The kiss he gave her was as gentle as his touch, but that wasn't what Stacey needed. She wanted it hard and fast. With sure movements she stroked his tongue again, captured it between her teeth and sucked, did her damnedest to show him what she wanted. Now.

Without breaking the kiss, Grant settled the tip of his

cock at her entrance, and in one hard thrust he was inside her.

She gasped at the pure pleasure of it, of the feel of him filling her completely before he pulled back. He plunged into her again and rotated his hips. Tension built, heightened her senses, her awareness, the feelings too intense, too powerful to ignore. "Oh, God."

"That's it," he coaxed. "Let go."

Like anything could stop her at this point. The man did incredible things with his hips, varying his thrusts so he held her on the edge of anticipation each time he pulled back.

She couldn't fight it any longer, couldn't prolong the inevitable, didn't want to.

The world tilted, flashing a kaleidoscope of vivid colors. She arched toward him, her groan mingling with his as he followed her over the edge.

# Chapter Twelve

Grant pulled Stacey to him, held her tight as their breathing slowed and they drifted back to earth. A thin sheen of sweat covered their bodies and it wasn't long before she shivered against him. Without a word he turned them both until she lay beside him.

He gently eased out of her, and her eyes opened. "Where are you going?"

"I'll be back. Let me take care of this." But somehow he couldn't move. There was something about the moment, something about her gaze latched onto his that made him stop, made him want to assure her that he truly would be back. And he wanted, he *needed*, to know she was okay with it. Only when she nodded did he break contact.

By the time he returned, Stacey was underneath the covers. Too bad she couldn't sit naked. He liked her that way. A lot.

"Hey," he said, the bed shifting under his weight.

"Mmmm…hey." She scooted over onto her side and laid her face on the pillow.

"You look spent, kind of like you...maybe enjoyed that." He grinned. It didn't take a scientist to figure that out, not when the smile on her face bloomed. She had a nice smile, a pretty smile, one that he'd grown accustomed to seeing over the years, but had he really *seen* it?

"I don't know." She turned her head and captured his gaze. "Seems to me you need more practice."

"Oh, really?"

"Well, yeah." She raised up onto her elbows, a mischievous light in her eyes that matched the whisper of a smile on her face. "That's the only way to get to perfect, don't you think?"

Another time, another place, this kind of banter with Stacey would've been normal. But after sex? In his experience most of the women he dated wanted to be cuddled, not get into a verbal sparring match. It was...refreshing.

He could get used to this. Permanently.

Wait. Permanently?

His body flashed hot, then cold.

Stacey frowned. "What's the matter?"

"Nothing." He willed some sense into his endorphin-filled brain.

Everything. Everything was wrong.

What the fuck had they just done?

And more importantly, had he just ruined everything?

...

Stacey yawned. She felt deliciously relaxed, her body free of tension so she was almost weightless. Great sex had a tendency to do that to her. Mind-blowing sex, on the other hand... She smiled. Guess she'd have to see how she recovered from it.

She pulled the comforter tighter around her and sighed. "I knew you had a lot of talents, Grant, but who knew Sex God was one of them?"

Whoa, what? Her eyes fluttered open as the words smacked her. Hard.

Grant. Bed. Naked. Totally and completely sated.

Holy hell. She'd just fucked Grant. Her best friend since forever. Not that sleeping with him once would change that, right? Didn't people hook up for a night and go back to normal the next day? Could they do that? Could *she* do it?

Stacey rolled out of bed, found her panties, and slid them on.

"What are you doing?"

"Painting my toenails. What does it look like I'm doing?" She found her bra on the bed but stopped when Grant effectively pinned it down with one hand. "Do you mind?"

Instead of the amusement she'd expected, there was a serious frown on his face. "We need to talk."

"About?" She shivered and then hugged her arms.

He pulled himself into a sitting position and patted the bed beside him. "Sit."

"I'm not sure I like your tone."

"Then sit and I'll quit using it." He patted the bed again. It was the same spot where she'd only moments before begged him to plunge into her.

*Oh. My. God.*

Stacey sat and bit her lower lip to stop the memories from running unchecked, from taking over reality altogether. But there was no way she could ignore the moisture seeping between her legs, or the way her body gently hummed because of what they'd just done.

He grabbed the afghan off the foot of the bed and gently placed it around her shoulders, the gesture achingly sweet. When was the last time any guy had thought about her comfort? Had cared enough to make her feel like she mattered?

Then again, this was Grant. He did stuff like this all the

time. It didn't necessarily mean anything.

He pulled her up against him. Exactly the way he had on the sofa, before the sex thing happened. Only now things were different. Way different.

She heaved in a deep breath and let it out slowly. There had to be something good that would come of this, although at the moment she was clueless as to what that might be, considering she'd just fucked her best friend.

He reached a hand onto her shoulder and lightly massaged it. "That was amazing."

She blinked up at him. His words were softly spoken, like he was awed by the experience. Wasn't he freaking out? Didn't he understand the gravity of what they'd just done?

"Yeah, it was." She leaned her head on his shoulder, his warmth soothing her in the same way it always had. "But now what? We just crossed the friend barrier." Certainly he realized that.

"Who says?"

"What do you mean?" She huffed out a breath. "We're clearly more than friends now, and yet we're *not* more than friends."

Oh, shit. She wasn't sure what the hell she'd just said.

"Do you regret what just happened?"

The question was quietly spoken, the words a soft-tipped spear aimed at her heart. Leave it to Grant to choose now to ask the most important question.

"No." That was the truth. "No, I don't. It was…amazing." She'd felt cherished and protected and safe, all things she'd not felt in a long time with a guy, if ever.

"Then why make this complicated?" He shifted until he partially faced her. "Why not enjoy what we've got?"

"Which is what, exactly?"

He shrugged. "I don't know, to be honest. But I do know that we've always been close. We shouldn't let something like having sex change that for us. I think it'd be sad if we do."

Maybe from his viewpoint. From where she was sitting, she was almost sure that cutting things off was better now than later. At least if they did it now, eventually her body would forget, wouldn't it? Then they could relax back into their easygoing relationship. Assuming that was still possible.

She sighed and dropped her head into her hands. This whole thing was confusing. And it was her own damned fault.

He pulled her close and planted a kiss on her forehead. "Nothing between us has to change. We're still best friends." He said it with such determination, such conviction, she half wondered if he was trying to convince himself. "If you're not comfortable adding sex to the equation, we won't."

Well, when he put it like that…

Walking away from their friendship didn't make sense, probably never would. They had too much invested in each other.

Whether or not they slept together again was an entirely different story.

"Best friends," she said, ignoring the little voice at the back of her head that told her tonight had been a bad idea. It was too late to go back now. At this point, Stacey wasn't sure she wanted to.

# Chapter Thirteen

"I don't know how you talked me into this," Stacey grumbled beside him. "I've got a ton of things to do today."

Grant pulled his kayak to the water's edge. This time of year, Spearhead Lake was typically quiet, particularly at midday. "You said yourself you've been working since seven this morning. You need a break and you know it."

"The water's going to be cold."

"Quit being a baby. We're only going to be in it long enough to get in and out." He straightened, placed fisted hands on his hips and stared at the top of her ball-capped head. "If I didn't know better, I'd say you're looking for any excuse not to enjoy this."

"Don't be ridiculous." She positioned her kayak alongside his, then adjusted her sunglasses. "It's a gorgeous day, the sun's out, tourist season hasn't really started. It's just that…"

"What? What's bothering you?"

"It feels weird. Like I want to hug you, but then that turns into kissing, and we both know where kissing gets us."

"Someplace fun?"

"Be serious."

"Are you trying to tell me last night wasn't fun? Maybe we should try it again, just to be sure." He kept a straight face, but his dick was definitely interested in her answer, particularly if he got the green light.

Her face turned the slightest shade of red. "That's not funny."

Grinning, he pulled her into his arms. "Here. Let's just get the hug thing out of the way so we can enjoy the afternoon."

"Goofball." She smacked him in the chest, but at least she'd relaxed some. "Fine."

He released her and turned his attention back to the kayaks. Another thirty seconds of that and he ran the risk of kissing her and proving her right. "Let's get our life vests on and hit the water."

A few minutes later they quietly paddled along the edge of the lake, the midday sun warm against his skin, and the life vest providing just enough warmth over his T-shirt.

"It's beautiful here." Stacey smiled, one end of her paddle dipping into the water and pulling her forward, her speed matching his. Not that he was going very fast. That was the thing about being out on the lake. Life slowed down enough that he felt grounded.

"Let's head over to Lava Cove and search for rocks," she suggested. "I'm putting a tablescape together for a client, so I could use some."

He nodded. Lava Cove was a popular spot on the other side of Spearhead Lake, and in the next few weeks, would play host to crowds of summer tourists. Today, it was likely empty.

Too bad it couldn't always be this way, but progress was progress, and the same crowd of tourists who took advantage of Milestone's outdoors also frequented the restaurants and bars that sold his distillery's whiskeys, bourbons, vodkas, and gins. Grant was more than happy to keep the stills working, the barrels filled, and the tourists happy.

He listened to the quiet, felt the rightness of the moment, felt the rightness of his life. There was something so *real* about all of it, here on the lake, with Stacey by his side. They didn't say much, didn't have to. It was one of the reasons he enjoyed her company, one of the many reasons they were best friends.

Julian's parting words drifted through his mind.

*"You treat Stacey right, and she'll be by your side your entire life…"*

As much as he needed them not to be true, he couldn't deny that there might be a kernel of truth hidden in their depths.

He was so screwed.

And he needed to slow things down before he screwed himself further.

. . .

"There." Stacey threw a handful of rocks into her plastic sack and stowed it in the kayak. "That should do it."

She smacked her arm. Damned mosquitos. Maybe she should throw on her life vest. Hard to get a tan that way, though.

Her stomach grumbled loud enough for Grant to hear it, confirmed a split second later when he pulled out the backpack he'd brought with him. "Sounds like it's time for food."

"What'd you bring?" She straddled the log opposite him, thankful that she'd pulled shorts over her bikini bottoms.

He handed her an apple. "I've got some nuts, too."

"I know that." Her eyes shot to his, and although she couldn't see through his sunglasses, she was willing to bet he was just as startled as she was by her words. "I mean, you always bring mixed nuts when we head out anywhere," she quickly added.

He shot her a lopsided grin. "And you seem to enjoy them."

"I do seem to have a thing for nuts," she agreed. A corner of her mouth tweaked up, and while she struggled with whether or not to voice her thoughts, she wasn't surprised when they won out in the end. "I especially like the kind that come in pairs."

He chuckled, the sound a caress over her warm skin. "Is that an invitation?"

"That depends. Are we flirting?"

"It would appear that way." He picked out a match, the flame bursting to life when he struck it against the side of the box.

"You brought candles." She grinned. "Are you sure this isn't a date?" she asked before biting into her apple.

"Do you want it to be?"

She stared out onto the lake as she chewed. Another time, another place, another guy, it'd be the perfect setting. Why couldn't it be the perfect setting now?

He grinned. "Hey, I was just kidding," he said, stowing the matchbox. "The candle's citronella. You know, to keep the bugs away. It's not exactly romantic."

"It's thoughtful. There's an element of romance in that."

Okay, what was going on here? Was she actually *trying* to make him fit her definition of someone romantic?

Geez. That was pathetic. Absolutely pathetic. This was Grant, for God's sake. Commitment-phobe, live-in-the-moment Grant. Not some hero out of a Hallmark movie.

"Look, Stace," he said, hands on his thighs. "I…um, that is… "

"Spit it out already."

He blew out a breath and stared across the lake. "You

know I want you to be happy, right? You know that means everything to me."

*Uh-oh.* He was trying to be serious, and her gut told her it wasn't a good thing.

"Yes." She took another bite of her apple to stop herself from saying more.

"As much fun as this is, and as much as I'd love to stay on the 'see where this goes' train, I don't want to see whatever this thing is between us get in the way of your finding the kind of guy who'd love you the way you want, the way you deserve."

And there it was. The biggest reason this was far from a Hallmark movie.

But as much as she wanted to challenge him, to point out all the ways they were good together, she knew he meant what he said. He wanted her to continue her search for another man. He didn't want her, at least not long term, and she respected herself far too much to argue for a relationship she knew he wasn't ready for.

A strange pang started in her chest and radiated outward. She chewed the apple slowly, its once sweet flavor falling flat.

He had abandonment issues, and while there were no guarantees in life, he had to have faith that not every woman was going to leave him. Unfortunately, she couldn't wave a magic wand and give him that faith. Every YouTube video she'd seen on the subject made it very clear that he had to do the work himself if he wanted to live a deeper, more fulfilling life. Which pretty much meant that, in this moment, he was who he was.

*So quit trying to make him something he's not.*

"Stace? You okay?"

"Of course." She waved him off with one hand. "Just thinking about my schedule. You know, where I'm going and what kind of guys might be there for me."

God, she hated lying, but now that she thought of it again, what was so wrong with going back to online dating? Some of the guys were questionable, but there was no rule that said she had to meet them. At the very least the experience would get her back in the dating game and her focus on someone besides Grant.

"How's your kayak working?" he asked, bringing her right back to Spearhead Lake and the apple she'd stopped munching on.

In light of their heavy conversation, it was a weird question.

Stacey took a deep breath and smiled as brightly as she could. "It's not taking in water, so it seems fine to me."

"I was thinking I'd like to take them on vacation with me one of these days."

"Wouldn't it be easier to just rent a kayak wherever you end up?" She kept her voice light, unaffected. It was the best way to get through this, to shine the proverbial light on their pseudo-relationship so she'd remember what it really was: temporary.

"Not every lake has someplace close by where I could do that. Besides," he added. "I thought I'd load them up, then take a road trip to Alaska next summer. Maybe stop along whatever lake or river I wanted and get in the water."

"Alaska, huh? What's the attraction?"

"Never been there before." He shrugged. "I just thought it sounded like a good idea."

Alaska.

With no invitation to join him.

They'd barely started, and he was already moving on.

Which meant Stacey had to figure out a way to do the same.

• • •

The crowds were bigger than they were at the mayor's brunch last week, which was likely the reason why Grant felt like he was suffocating. He tugged at the noose around his neck. Okay, it was a tie, but same difference.

Hard to believe some guys wore a tuxedo on a regular basis…by choice. He, on the other hand, had been suckered to parade around in something that wasn't shorts and a T-shirt for the second time in two weeks.

Although Stacey *had* mentioned how nice he looked tonight. He scanned the ballroom and frowned. She'd disappeared into the crowd almost as soon as they'd arrived, but in a room full of eligible bachelors, it wasn't hard to guess what she was doing.

His frown deepened. What did it matter to him? He'd been the one to tell her she needed to continue her manhunt. It was in her own best interest. He wouldn't be a dick and tell her she couldn't.

"Grant? Is that really you?"

The familiar voice broke through his thoughts, made the hairs on the back of his neck prickle even before he turned around. And speaking about life happening… "Trisha."

His ex. A woman he'd dated much longer than he should have. It shouldn't have surprised him to see the beautiful blonde here. The Milestone Moments Gala was the area's premiere event, and the woman had always aimed high—which was a big reason they didn't work out.

"Don't you look good." She didn't bother to cover her purr of admiration and swept her gaze up and down him like he was a fur coat she wanted to slide her arms into. "Glad to see you've taken my advice and upgraded your wardrobe."

Grant frowned. Clearly not much had changed.

She took half a step back and tossed her blonde hair to the side in a way that he'd once thought sexy and inviting. Now he couldn't wait to ditch her.

Trisha scanned him from top to bottom and back again. "What are you wearing? Hugo Boss?" She eyed him critically. "You've got the right frame for it."

Hugo Boss? Hell if he knew. The distillery's marketing manager had shown up at his office last week with a suit bag and orders to wear it tonight. Oh, he'd protested. Same as with the suit a couple weeks ago. His board shorts and T-shirt were a truer reflection of the kinds of clothes worn by the market they were targeting—the easygoing, relaxed, kick-back-after-work crowd. But Kylie was right. He couldn't ignore the older, more sophisticated crowd, either.

"Yes, that's Hugo Boss," she said before he could answer. "I'd recognize a Hugo Boss anywhere."

Apparently, he didn't need to be around to participate in her conversation.

"I heard you're part owner at Mile High Desert Distillery now." Trisha's blue eyes glimmered with interest. No doubt it had more to do with his new position at the distillery, a place she'd once referred to as his dead-end job.

"I am." On the one hand, it was weird that he felt no need to gloat, but the truth was that Trisha no longer mattered, her opinions no longer mattered.

When he turned, he caught his reflection in the mirrored wall at one side of the room. Hugo Boss or not, he had to admit the tux looked good on him. Too bad he didn't give a damn about any of it. Stacey would probably insist that although he cleaned up well, it simply wasn't who he was.

A splotch of bright pink reflected off the mirror, and his heartbeat kicked up. She was at the far end of the room, and he openly admired her in much the same way when he'd picked her up. The low-cut, backless gown she wore was a sexy blend of innocence and temptress.

She was light and perfection, happiness and kindness and caring wrapped in a sexy package. She made him believe, for one tiny moment, that he was part of something larger, something better, something far more satisfying than being alone.

A trace of irritation ran through him. It was likely due to Trisha jabbering at him about her latest real estate brokerage sale and the huge commission. It definitely wasn't because Stacey seemed to be involved in a deep conversation with some relatively good-looking guy. Feeling territorial was plain stupid. She deserved to be happy, even if he wasn't part of that equation.

His gaze flickered back to the blonde, and, not bothering to wait for a break in her one-sided conversation, he said, "You take care, Trisha. Gotta go."

He swirled the glass of bourbon in his hand and walked away. He fought the temptation to tug at his bow tie one more time and scanned the crowd again. Where'd Stacey go?

Ever since the kayaking trip, they'd managed to get back to the easygoing relationship they'd always had. Thank God. Every time he thought about the possibility of losing her, his stomach churned. What a relief he hadn't lost her, that they were still friends. And he'd made damned sure he kept his hands and his dick to himself from that point on.

"There you are." Stacey came up behind him, a smile on her pretty face. Errant strands of hair fell forward, and he itched to tuck them back, to skim a hand across the planes of her smooth face...to lean forward and kiss her...

*Keep your hands to yourself.* And his lips, too, if he knew what was good for him.

The reminder had him shoving his free hand in his pocket while the other brought his glass to his mouth.

Oblivious to his inner turmoil, she casually looked around. "So, I see your ex is here tonight. How is she?"

"Fine, I guess." He searched her face. Clearly, she'd adjusted well to going back to their best-friend status. Sex must not have affected her as much as he'd expected.

Why did that bother him so much? He should be grateful that sex hadn't affected her, that she didn't obsess about it, or turn all pouty and moody when they took a step back.

Wait. That wasn't exactly something a guy should be proud of, was it?

Didn't matter. Grant wouldn't freak. It wasn't his place, and likely would earn him a tongue lashing at the least. Not the good kind, either.

"One thing I've never understood," Stacey began, her brown eyes boring into his. "You've got all these commitment issues, and yet you hung onto *her* way longer than you should've. What's up with that?"

He scowled. "That was all your fault."

"My fault?" She raised an eyebrow, almost daring him to speak. "Oh, this I've got to hear. The woman was a leech, looking at your potential versus who you really are. She wanted you at her beck and call, and when you didn't give her attention, she'd blow up on you. How was any of that even *remotely* my fault? Really." She sniffed. "I thought you had better taste than that."

"You were the one who lectured me about giving a woman a chance."

"After you quit dating a woman because she wanted to do nice things for you like make you dinner or do your laundry," she pointed out. "Believe me, if some woman offered to cook for me or do my laundry, I'd keep her around, not label her as 'too clingy,' then drop her like last week's bad advice. But that still doesn't explain why you hung onto Trisha."

"She was just the next woman to walk into my life after you tore into me about giving women a chance."

She raised an eyebrow. "That's it? That's the reason you stuck with her? I'm not sure if I should laugh or cry."

"Neither. I followed your advice. I wasn't what she

wanted. Story of my life." He kept his tone light, unaffected, never mind the painful stab of emotion in his chest.

Plastering on a smile, he thumbed at the room behind him. "You having a good time tonight?"

Her face morphed into a huge grin, excitement glimmering in her eyes while she took a quick sip of her champagne. "I made some great contacts for Dinners for Two, but the best news? I just nailed myself a new client who's amazingly generous."

Clients…networking…not a manhunt. Relief washed through him, so much so that he relaxed his shoulders and grinned. "Yeah? What makes him so generous?"

"Not just what he's willing to spend, but who he's arranging the dinner for." She tilted her head to one side. "And, I haven't had guys do this sort of thing, but he's offering a thirty percent gratuity and a write-up in a Pacific Northwest e-zine. Pretty neat, huh?"

"That'd be great exposure for you. Congratulations." He pasted on a smile. "Who's the guy?"

Stacey's sparkling brown eyes widened. "He wants his identity to remain anonymous," she said.

"Why bother to keep it such a secret?"

"It's more romantic that way, silly." She huffed out a breath. "Of course, he said that I could shout it from the top of Chinaman Hat if things go smoothly."

He frowned. Obviously, the guy thought there was a good chance he'd strike out, but at least Stacey had landed a new client. Why shouldn't she be excited? She worked damned hard and poured her heart and soul into what she did. She had a passion that was rarely seen in most people.

She had a passion for everything she touched. And her passion *fed* everything she touched. Especially when she touched him.

Grant stared at her upturned face, her eyes all sparkly

and her mouth curved into that blend of mischievous and sexy that belonged only to her.

*Awww, hell…*

He caved. Despite all the mental arguments he'd had with himself, he reached for Stacey, his hand sliding over her bare arm. Skin on skin contact—he needed it, drowned in it. He hadn't realized until this moment how much he'd missed holding her, missed the feel of her in his arms.

Hot and cold flashes undulated through his body like Klaxon alarms. What the hell was he thinking? But even as the thought raced through his brain, he knew.

Stacey was perfect for him.

That thought swirled around his head, nipped at his psyche and pulled back, a strange mix of emotions hot on its trail.

"You okay?" The slight frown on her face and the concern in her voice tipped him over the edge. She looked past him at the crowd. "You've already done your bit for the distillery, so I'm okay to leave if you are."

Oh, he wanted to leave all right, but not for the reasons she was thinking. Grant tugged her toward him, wrapped his arm around her waist, and pressed her to him. Surprise registered in her eyes when she turned her face up.

In one slow move, Grant lowered his head and captured her mouth in a soft, reverent kiss. The way she deserved.

...

His mouth was firm, gentle, coaxing rather than demanding, and brief. Stacey had barely closed her eyes when he pulled away and teased her with an equally gentle smile.

She stared, mesmerized by the curve of his lips, by the playfulness in his eyes, by the way he softly caressed her face. She wanted to taste him, wanted to feel him, all of him. She wanted to give herself up to the moment and just *be*.

Stacey blinked. Blood thrummed in her ears and pulsed through her temples. That was something she hadn't experienced before with Grant, and definitely not with any other man. It was good. Too good. Not possessive, yet possessing every sensory system in her body so that she was attuned to this man, this moment.

Damn.

"Considering we have a bit of an audience, we should probably hang out awhile longer," he said.

An audience?

She glanced behind her at a couple of blue-haired women who stood off to the side. Their raised eyebrows and polite smiles made it painfully clear they were eavesdropping. Stacey turned away and pushed him back as she walked forward, effectively moving them away from the women. "Who cares what they think?" she asked when they were a few feet away.

He cupped her face briefly, then tucked a strand of hair behind one ear. "Normally, I wouldn't. But those two own Milestone Media." He squeezed her hand. "They could probably run a story on you one day, and as conservative as they are, I'm guessing the last thing you want is to give them the impression that you're unprofessional because you publicly sucked face."

"Good point." Milestone was pretty progressive as a whole, but acting in a less-than-serious-businesswoman mode probably wasn't in the best interest of her business.

"C'mon," he said. "Let's get fresh glasses."

Glasses? She looked at the champagne flute in her hand. Good God, she was seriously losing it.

He guided her toward the bar, one hand placed on the small of her back. And not for the first time that evening, she was glad she'd chosen a backless gown, one that dipped just below her waist. The warmth of his hand seared her, branded her in much the same way his kiss had just moments before.

And in a flash it dawned on her. She'd known Grant since they were kids, knew every secret he had, every battle he'd fought, and had even fought alongside him in some cases. But she'd never been prepared for the possibility that the hardest battle she'd have to fight was the one waging inside her now.

With one sweet kiss, he'd torn down every defense she believed she'd possessed, every shred of logic that told her their friendship was all they had, all she could hope for.

Stacey stared straight ahead and swallowed back the tide of longing.

Dear God. She was so in trouble with this man.

And she suspected she'd enjoy every minute of it.

# Chapter Fourteen

Grant stood outside Stacey's door. The six-pack of beer he had with him was normal, the bouquet of flowers he clutched was not. He frowned. The flowers were just an afterthought when he picked up the beer. That was all.

Then again, maybe the flowers were overkill. He should ditch them. Unfortunately, his only option was to toss them over the stairway that led to her third-floor apartment.

He gave himself a mental shake. *Stop. Slow down. Think.*

He was acting like an idiot. This was Stacey, for God's sake. Her invitation tonight was some sort of an emergency. Something about testing out a last-minute recipe. Which was weird, to be honest. Carly normally tested recipes, not Stacey. Then again, knowing Stacey, she probably wanted to prove she could cook, that cooking was just another language she could learn by simply following a recipe, as she liked to say.

So how come he was so fucking nervous?

He sucked in some air and blew it out slowly. The two of them had been tight for years. What the hell was he so afraid of?

He knocked on the door before turning the knob and walking in. "Hey," he called out. "I'm here."

"In the kitchen."

The smells were fragrant. He walked into the kitchen, his mouth watering, then stopped.

She was barefoot at the stove with her back to him. Her dress fell to mid-thigh, exposing firm, creamy skin. "Hey." She glanced over her shoulder and her gaze landed on the bouquet in his hands. "You brought tulips."

The appreciation in her voice tugged at his heart and challenged his sensibilities.

"Yeah, well..." He searched his brain for some smart-mouth comeback, something that would throw her off, throw the conversation off. It was either that or acknowledge that many other men were on to something with the whole romance thing. Or replay what it'd been like to have her legs wrapped around him when he took her home after the charity ball.

Damn.

If he was going to make it through dinner, he'd have to get past thinking about her naked. Well, maybe with a pair of panties on...and heels. Like the kind she'd worn that night. She'd kept them on long after he'd undressed her...

What the fuck? He mentally shook his head. *Not helpful, buddy.*

"Let me take those from you." She crossed the short distance between them and took the bouquet. "I love tulips." There was that shine in her eyes again. He'd never get tired of seeing it, and he'd never get tired of putting it there, either. Why hadn't he brought her flowers before?

"What's the big emergency?" he asked, setting the six-pack down.

"My new client." She opened a cabinet underneath the sink and bent over, the hem of her dress inching up so it barely covered her ass. "I think I've got a vase in here somewhere."

*Nice view.* "I bet it's way in the back. Might even have to get on your hands and knees and dig for it." He grinned.

She wiggled her cute ass at him before straightening with a vase in hand. "Nice try, goofball."

She said the words but the sarcasm was clearly missing.

"What's for dinner?" He grabbed a beer, then searched through a drawer for the bottle opener. "I hope it goes with beer."

"It'll go with beer." She placed the vase on the counter.

"You sure? Because your clients usually want those two-bite kinds of food."

She remained silent, which was just plain weird for Stacey.

"Look," he said, "if it's a two-bite kind of thing, it'll be okay. I promise."

She stood with her back to him as she arranged the flowers in the vase. "About that…ummm…there is no client."

No client. He frowned. "So, dinner tonight…"

"Is because I wanted to." She turned around and shrugged, and there was that hint of insecurity again, the kind that made him want to have her in his arms, telling her it'd be okay. "I wanted to make dinner for you."

He felt his eyes go wide. "You did?"

She shrugged. "Yeah, I wanted to do something special, so I figured I could make you dinner."

He wasn't sure what shocked him more, that she'd made dinner or that he actually planned to eat it. After all, it wasn't like cooking was her forte.

"I guess you're finally using that cookbook I got you for Christmas three years ago," he blurted.

*Brilliant. Fucking brilliant.* Okay, it wasn't exactly what he was going for, but there was no way to take it back now.

There was a strange look on her face, almost like she wasn't sure what to say.

"I meant," he started. "You've talked about cooking a lot, so I'm glad you're getting into it."

She sucked in a deep breath, her gaze locked onto his, and then nodded, like she'd reached a conclusion. "Come." She took his hand and led him through the kitchen to the dining area. "I wanted to... I mean, it seemed like... God, I don't know. Maybe this was a bad idea."

He frowned. What had her so flustered? The question barely registered when his eyes landed on the small table, its center occupied by a miniature racetrack and a lone red car. Just like the one he'd played with when life was simpler, when all he'd had to worry about was keeping it away from his younger brother.

A well of emotion pierced the center of his chest, the memories tumbling forward and crashing past the barriers he'd erected since that afternoon his mother had dropped him off to play. Before she got in her beat-up sedan and drove off.

It wasn't until that moment that he'd felt the fear as he chased after the car, that clawing, strangling sensation that threatened to overwhelm him, take him under, and keep him there. He'd run as fast as an eight-year-old's legs could take him, stopping only when the social worker had grabbed the back of his shirt and yanked him off the street.

He reached a hand out and tentatively touched the red racecar, the metal cool under his fingertips. It was a long time ago, and even though he'd spent the better part of his childhood being shuffled between foster care homes, he knew he was better off just rolling with life than struggling against it. He swallowed past the lump in his throat, swallowed down the fear, the pain, the loneliness.

"Where... How..." Great. Now *he* couldn't string a simple sentence together.

"Took me a while to find it," she said quietly. "I got this

online. It just came in today."

He turned to face her. "But why?"

She wrapped her arms around herself, looking so damned vulnerable he wanted to gather her in his arms. "Sometimes the best way to face the future is to embrace the past and recognize it's a part of who we are, you know? The past shaped you into the warm, caring person you are today, Grant. I thought you should know that."

Had it shaped him? Given his childhood start, maybe that was true. But to examine it now...well, that wasn't something he was ready to take on. Not when a beautiful, caring woman had gone through all the trouble of making a special meal for him. No matter what it tasted like, he'd eat it. "You went through all this trouble for me?"

"Trouble? Are you kidding me? You've helped with my business, and you were great with Julian and Martha..." She shrugged. "I just felt like doing something nice for you." She glanced at the table. "I hope it's okay."

He followed her gaze, recognition burning into him when he spotted a kayak at the base of a candleholder, the racetrack encircling it. Underneath it all was a map. He angled his head to get a better look.

"Alaska?" He alternated his attention between each item and the tentative smile on Stacey's face.

"The racetrack's from your past, the kayak is your present, and the map of Alaska...well, I can't possibly know what your future looks like, but you mentioned taking a road trip through there, so I thought..."

All he could do was stare. No one had ever put together something so thoughtful for him before. No one. And then it struck him as plainly as a peaceful day on Spearhead Lake: she brought into this moment the kinds of things that made him happy, things that reminded him to savor what was most important in life.

He took a deep breath, did his damnedest to infuse the memory into every cell in his body. Only someone special would do something like this for him. That's exactly who Stacey was. Someone special.

He grinned. "It's more than okay, Stace. It's perfect."

. . .

Stacey bit down on her lower lip. Thank God her instincts were on target with the whole dinner idea, because it was only now that her head acknowledged what her heart had known all along. Grant was important to her. Deeply, irrevocably important in more than the best-friend-since-they-were-kids way.

Their gazes locked, and a thrill shot through her, zipping past her defenses so she was totally focused on this man, this moment. She took a deep breath and indicated the table with one hand. "Put some music on, and I'll get dinner on the table."

"Don't you want help?"

"Oh, no, I've got it. It won't take me long." She'd probably burn in hell for lying about making the food, but she'd seen the pleasure on Grant's face when he'd thought she had actually cooked tonight. No way she'd disappoint him now.

She opened the oven door and pulled out the tray with individual chicken potpies on them. Carly had said to make sure to bake them until the crust was brown. Was this brown enough? She searched her memory for some reference point for brown and came up empty.

It was as brown as a paper bag. Was that what she meant?

Ugh. Stacey needed to take her sister's advice and exude confidence. This was just food, for Pete's sake. She ate the stuff, so she didn't need to make it any more complicated than it already was. Still, maybe she should text her sister.

"What'd you make?"

Startled, she dropped her phone, catching it just before it fell onto the tiled floor. "Don't scare me like that." She set the phone facedown on the counter. So much for getting Carly's opinion.

"Sorry," Grant said, stepping into the kitchen. "It just smells so good in here."

"These are chicken potpies." She arranged them on dinner plates. "I hope you're hungry." She stuffed down the temptation to own up to the fact she didn't make them. After all, what harm could actually come from it? And one day she really would learn to cook. Maybe.

"Smells good." He smiled. "You sure I can't help with anything?"

Well, shoot, if the man was going to insist, why not? "Salad's in the fridge if you'd like to bring it out."

And it was just like it always was, the two of them working side by side, laughing and joking so that by the time everything was on the table, she was pretty sure the evening would be perfect.

"You know something? I get it," he said. His voice softened and he smiled. "I totally get it now."

"Huh?" She tilted her head to one side and frowned. "Sorry. You lost me there."

"This. All of this." He spread his arms wide. "What you do for other people, how you set up these dinners. You create memories for them. Good memories."

She arched an eyebrow. "I thought you knew that. You mentioned it when I told you about Julian."

"I know, but I was trying to make you feel better. I didn't really get it. Until now."

"Well, I suppose that's the general idea. But it really depends on the client. Sometimes it's just as important to connect the present to the future. You know, to build on the strength of a relationship so there's enough to fuel it forward." At least, that's what'd made sense to her, and she had repeat business to back her up.

"You're really good at what you do. You know that, don't you?"

She blinked, a well of emotion opening up inside her and bubbling out. It was validation. One she'd needed to hear badly from him, only she hadn't realized it until now. Warmth spread through her, the moment stamped onto her as powerfully as sunshine on a summer day. "Thank you."

He turned his attention back to the tablescape she'd created, and the steaming chicken potpie in front of him. "Thank *you*." He shook his head. "This is amazing."

"You're welcome." There was that warmth thing going on again. If she wasn't careful, she'd combust.

Maybe their relationship *could* evolve. Even if he'd nudged her in the direction of finding a long-term relationship, maybe he believed it enough to give it a shot? She huffed out a mental breath. She was typically optimistic, but with Grant? He was a wild card.

Okay, so maybe she should stop daydreaming and just enjoy whatever they had for however long it lasted. Because there was a better than fair chance their relationship *wouldn't* evolve beyond the friends-who-fuck stage.

"So, how'd you make this?"

*Oh, shit.* Why hadn't she been prepared for Grant to ask questions? She shoved a forkful of hot pie in her mouth, then felt her eyes widen. The pie tasted…funny…like a part of it was burned. Which was weird. She'd followed her sister's instructions carefully. Carly must've given her the wrong directions or temperature or something. Or maybe "brown" was lighter than she expected. But how to salvage it now?

"You okay?" He leaned toward her, a concerned frown on his face.

"Hot," she managed, blowing on her food. Unfortunately, that didn't work as well when said food was already in her mouth. But at least it saved her from having to answer right away. She reached for her glass of white wine and took a sip. At least the wine was cold, even though it didn't do much to ease the burn. This was probably cosmic justice at work for lying about making dinner.

He carefully shoved a spoonful in his mouth, chewed, then flashed a frown. "I taste something different about this. Ummm... It's really good. What's in it?"

Correction. His question was cosmic justice. She carefully placed her fork down. "It's...ummm...something Carly recommended I use. Said it added an herby quality to the filling."

"Herby, huh?" Grant nodded, tilting his head to one side as if considering how to respond. "Which one?"

"Which one?" Oh, shit. Unfortunately, parsley was about the only herb she knew. Basil? That was an herb, too, right? Did basil go in a chicken potpie? "Ummm...it's a...ummm... secret green herb."

"I see. Can you at least give me a hint?"

She took a long sip of her wine and tried desperately to come up with something, anything that sounded remotely like it belonged in a chicken potpie. Then she glanced in his direction, saw the corners of his mouth twitch up like he was trying to contain his laughter.

"You know, don't you?"

"Know what?" His eyes twinkled.

"Don't toy with me, Grant. You know I didn't make this."

He chuckled. "It was a pretty easy deduction, really."

"What do you mean?"

"Your kitchen's clean."

"So? Maybe I cleaned it up before you came over."

"And when I tossed the bottle cap, there wasn't anything

in your garbage to indicate you'd so much as opened a can, let alone cooked chicken."

"Maybe I threw the trash out before you came over."

"Why? You usually have me do that when I leave."

*Damn. Damn. Double damn.*

"You're entirely too observant."

"That's not a crime."

The half smile on his face seemed to be contagious, and before long she couldn't stop her own smile if her life had depended on it.

"Lastly," he added, his smile morphing into an all-out grin. "Secret green herb? Really? You could've at least said parsley or something."

*Damn!* She should've trusted her gut and gone with parsley.

"Hey, at least I tried."

His smile faded, replaced by something deeper, something she couldn't quite put her finger on. "You did better than try, Stacey. This is amazing. *You're* amazing."

"I burned it."

He shrugged as if it didn't matter to him. "It tastes fine to me."

She arched an eyebrow. "Liar."

He reached across the table and grasped her hand. "This is the most amazing experiences anyone has ever given me, Stace. I promise I'm not lying about that."

A shock of electricity bolted through her, starting with her chest and moving in tingly waves through her body. There he went with the validation again. Something about this man, this moment, would be forever imprinted on her brain. She wasn't sure what it was, but she'd bask in it for as long as it was around.

By the time the last of the dinner dishes were put away, Stacey was still running on adrenaline. It was like every part of reality was magnified somehow.

She openly admired his profile while he loaded up the dishwasher. What was it about him that made her feel... incredible? Like she could accomplish anything, could follow whatever path she chose.

How bad was it, really, that they'd stepped beyond the realm of friendship into something deeper? Something even more intimate than the closeness they already shared?

Sure, it might've started out awkwardly, but she didn't feel that way anymore. Now it felt normal, and that was a good thing. It meant that maybe, just maybe, they'd grow their friendship instead of lose it. After all, sex was supposed to deepen intimacy, wasn't it? She shrugged to herself. At least, she'd remembered reading that on a relationship blog.

"What are you thinking?" Grant asked before he blew out the candles so that the only light came from the corner lamp. "You shrugged," he added at her raised eyebrow. "Must've been something pretty deep."

Well, if she wanted to grow their relationship, what better time to start than now?

"Oh, it was deep, all right." She tilted her head to one side and grinned. "I suppose you could say that it's *way* deep..."

Desire flashed in his eyes, and that *something* between them sparked and came to life. She felt the trace of warmth as it circled her, seemingly anchoring itself around her and pulling ever so slightly.

"Come here."

She raised an eyebrow even as she approached him. He thought he was in command of this part of the night? Not. Even.

Time to get this party going. She slowed her pace, kept it in time to the beat of Lady Gaga blasting out of the speakers, then stopped. Rocking her hips from side to side, she watched the small smile register on his face. With one hand, she reached around to the back of her dress, found the metal tab, and tugged it down.

Grant stood rigid, his gaze intensely focused on her movements. "This is another surprise," he murmured.

"Why?" She turned her back to him, spread her legs wide, and let the music move her body again. "I like this song." She peeked over her shoulder and winked.

"I just never figured you for the striptease type."

"Really?" She pulled the tab lower, doing her best to imitate a woman bent on seducing her man. Although in this case, it was a fair bet she wouldn't have to work too hard.

"Really."

Was that a hitch in his voice? Good. The tone empowered her further, spurred her on so that she lowered the zipper to the bottom before dropping her shoulders and slowly letting the material slide down her body.

She caught the dress so it covered her breasts, then spun around to face him.

He was staring, his arms crossed, and his face giving nothing away. That is, unless she counted the way his eyes darkened, the pupils dilated. Or the way he swallowed deeply and looked like every ounce of him was exercising restraint.

And she loved every minute of it.

"You gonna keep going, or just stand there teasing me?" There was an edge to his voice despite his cool, calm, collected exterior. "Or maybe you want me to help?"

"Uh-uh." She shook her head, gyrated her hips and slowly inched the material down. It slid over the tops of her breasts, brushed against her bare nipples, teasing them into hard points. "Mmmm…"

He swallowed, and energy seemed to burst from him. Restrained energy that combined with his dilated pupils and fisted hands. He was coiled tight, and she intended to tighten him up more before granting him release.

She looked pointedly at his crotch, at the way the fabric of his shorts stretched to accommodate him. "I think you're doing great standing right there. Besides, this is my show."

The dress slid over her hips, then she finally let go so the soft fabric fell to her feet, leaving her in nothing but a pair of her sexiest panties. She stepped out of them at the same moment Grant unfolded his arms.

He reached her in less than three strides, then pulled her into a rough embrace. She gasped. His mouth crushed down on hers. Passion overrode any semblance of logic that tried to take hold of her brain. How could it with the way his mouth claimed hers, demanded she give as well as take?

It didn't require much coaxing. She opened her mouth and their tongues danced. And it *was* a dance, wasn't it? The way he teased, retreated, came toward hers again and again like a secret code embedded in the rhythm of his movements, in the way he gently nipped and tugged.

His hands roamed over her back, her hips, and then, just as quickly as he started, he broke off the kiss. The movement had barely registered, the protest on her lips quickly replaced with surprise. "Hey."

Grant effortlessly hauled her over his shoulder. Sure, she was small, but she wasn't exactly used to being treated like a sack of potatoes, either. "Hey," she said again. "What are you doing?"

"Painting my toenails."

The words she'd once hurled at him came back at her now, and just like he'd done at the time, Stacey chuckled. "Maybe you need a few lessons in that department. I'd be glad to help."

His strides were long and sure, covering the length of her apartment until they were in her bedroom. He lowered her to the floor, her body achingly sliding along his. "Well, well," she teased, stroking a hand over his hard bulge. "What do we have here?"

He growled, a low, demanding sound that only fueled her blood and made her all the more determined to play the temptress to his caveman. "I'm pretty sure you know what's waiting for you."

His words ignited her, made her nipples tight and the bud between her legs throb. "You might have to remind me." She ran her fingers over his biceps, felt them flex.

Without another word he quickly pulled his shirt over his head. He unbuckled his belt next, pulled the tab of his shorts open, then stopped, his hands at his sides. "Finish it."

There was something about the command in his voice, about the look on his face, in his eyes, that reached out and tugged at her soul. He'd done a great job following her lead, but this time, he wanted to be in charge. And there was nothing hotter than a sexy man in charge.

She splayed a hand over his hard stomach, then dragged her fingers down until she reached the zipper. Slowly, she pulled the tab down over his hard ridge. "Oh, dear... Looks like it might be stuck." She released the tab and pressed her hand on his erection. "I might have to hold it in a bit to get the zipper down."

"Baby doll." He groaned the words out, half pain, half pleasure.

"What?" She threw him a quick glance. "Am I not allowed to cop a feel? Think of it like a fee for doing your bidding."

"Oh, I'll more than pay your fee." The promise was laced with a layer of thinly veiled lust. "And maybe even have you beg for more."

"I sure hope so."

# Chapter Fifteen

She was deliberately slowing things down, that much was clear.

Grant held his breath and kept his arms from reaching for Stacey's waist. It'd be so easy to grab her and tumble into bed with her on top. Sure, restraint was a good thing, but after spending most of the evening with one invisible cord binding his hands to himself, he had to admit it'd felt so damned good just to hold her.

She was inches away, a sexy smile on her face and one hand lightly touching his dick. A part of him wanted to press himself toward her, wanted to insist she hurry, but something was different tonight.

It had been bad enough when she'd first wiggled her cute ass at him, but he had no idea she could do a striptease act that would rival a pole dancer's moves. Not that he frequented strip clubs, but he'd been to bachelor parties over the years, and none of them had had the impact on him that Stacey's moves did tonight.

He fought back every male instinct to take control, but

that didn't mean he couldn't help things along, either.

"You planning to tease me all night?"

"*May*-be," she murmured softly, a sigh escaping her lips. Her eyes brightened and a smile pulled at the corners of her mouth. She sank to her knees, her gaze on his, and her hand still stroking his dick. "What have we got here?"

When she squeezed, he shuddered, closing his eyes.

Slow. Slow and easy. That's what he wanted with her tonight.

His senses were acutely tuned to Stacey and the way she stroked his dick before finally, *finally* pulling the zipper tab all the way down and releasing him.

"Mmmm…impressive…"

"Glad you approve."

Everything about her tonight ignited a spark in him. Her scent, her smile, the way she teasingly reached for the waistband of his boxer briefs and tugged the material the rest of the way down. His erection jutted out, proud and strong. "And I see you're ready for some action."

"With you, I'm always ready." He breathed the words out, barely hearing himself above the pounding of his heart.

It was true. Every intimate moment he'd spent with her, every kiss, every caress, even her soft snores in the middle of the night touched his heart, touched him deeply. He'd tried to keep those kinds of thoughts at bay, tried to inject some sanity into them, but why bother to deny it? Stacey was even more important to him than he'd first realized.

He reached for her, caressed her face, then slowly guided her up.

Stacey was his past. She was his present. And now that he was man enough to admit it to himself, she was his future, too.

With one soft kiss he knew it was time that he proved it.

•  •  •

The kiss was soft, sweet, not the hurried, frenzied kind she'd experienced with him before. Stacey couldn't quite put her finger on it, but something had shifted between them tonight. Something about the mood, about the feel of Grant on her as he slowly, almost reverently brought her body to life, kindled a spark soul deep.

Grant reached between them and stroked a thumb over her nipple before lowering his head to cover it with his tongue.

Stacey moaned. He made her feel like she had one foot in reality and the other in a mind-blowing world of pure sensation.

*Holy wow.*

Electric pulses arced through her, centering on the sensitive spot between her legs. She closed her eyes and allowed the pulses to cascade, circulating around her on a wave of emotion so intense, she wanted more.

She squirmed and leaned into him a bit harder, but he pulled back. "More," she gasped. "I want more."

"Soon, I promise."

She gritted her teeth, her body craving his touch, craving the pleasure only Grant could bring.

With each pass he came a millimeter closer to the spot that begged for him. Her eyes drifted shut, and she concentrated, willing him toward the spot she so wanted him to touch.

He hauled her upright and stood, taking her with him. Her eyes opened as she gripped his shoulders and wrapped her legs around his waist. "What are you doing?"

"Making it easier to get a condom on." He settled himself on the bed and she eagerly arranged her body on top of his, making sure his ridge was nestled in the perfect spot between her legs. From this angle she could move over him, coating him with her moisture. "This better?"

"God, yes." She sighed, leaned forward, and planted a kiss along his jawline. She did this to him. She made him hard, she made him want her. The knowledge was heady…powerful…humbling.

He reached into the nightstand, then handed her a foil packet. It didn't take long for her to tear open the package and sheath him. "Where were we?" she asked, straddling him again.

"I think you're in the right zip code."

With their gazes locked, Stacey lifted up and positioned the tip of his cock at her entrance. She bit her lower lip and pushed down and over him, then stopped. That first entry was always a thrill…a shock…a desire for more. She hissed out a breath, adjusting to his length and thickness.

Closing her eyes, she relished the rush of emotion tumbling through her, the lust that mixed with something she couldn't quite put a finger on, wasn't sure she even wanted to.

"Mmmm…" How was it possible that sex could be playful and fun as well as seriously intense? Or was it just that way with Grant? It certainly hadn't been with anyone else.

She opened her eyes, moved her hips forward, and rose slightly above him. Up and down and up and down… Grant filled her fully. Completely. They shared a rhythm that strummed at her soul, that made her believe in the *rightness* of this moment, at the possibility that maybe, just maybe, a lifetime of moments like this were possible with Grant. And just as she was getting used to the rhythm, to the feel of him in her, he held her tight, then quickly turned them both until he was on top of her.

"*Oh.*"

"You okay?" But even as he asked the question, he pumped deep inside her.

"Perfect."

There were no more words after that as his strokes first

lengthened, then shortened, catching her senses off guard and keeping her off-kilter so that the pressure built inside her, pushed her higher, harder, faster.

"You ready to come? I don't think I can hang on much longer." He gasped the words out, lowered his head, then gave her a hard kiss.

Tilting her hips, she let him in deeper still and the tension in her body multiplied, edging her even higher until, with one hard thrust from Grant, the world splintered, sending her down in a haze of fireworks.

With a long, loud groan he drove into her. "*Stacey.*"

He lowered his head until his forehead rested on hers, their breathing hard and fast.

"God, that was good," she finally whispered.

"Yeah, it was."

Would it always be this way between them? Like two lost lovers who'd found each other over a continent and a lifetime away? Didn't matter. None of it mattered beyond this moment. At least, that's what Grant would say.

Maybe it was time she believed it, too.

# Chapter Sixteen

Grant stared at the large, empty bins that would hold the mash for what would become the next batch of bourbon. He pulled the clipboard down and read through the notes. Whiskey. He was blending whiskey. The bourbon was already being distilled.

After the night he'd had with Stacey, focusing on anything but her was becoming a real challenge. Not that he minded the images drifting through his mind. Or what they were inspiring him to do the second he could get his hands on her again.

"You okay?"

Grant turned toward the voice. "Yeah." He waved off Patrick Donovan, one of his partners. "Why?"

"You seem pretty happy."

"I'm always happy."

Patrick raised an eyebrow, "I know you better than that."

Grant shrugged, but he couldn't wipe the smile from his face.

"Is this about a girl?"

"Yep."

"Well." Patrick pulled his glasses off and rubbed them

clean with the edge of his white T-shirt. "Don't let yourself get too distracted since, you know, you're behind production schedule."

Grant's smile faded, but he remained silent. Underneath the light tone was an underpinning of hard truth, one that his partner wouldn't let him miss.

One of the reasons Patrick was a shrewd businessman was his ability to read people. Whether one-on-one, or an entire population, he had this uncanny knack to gauge habits and form an intelligent business decision based on his observations. Grant had watched him do it since college. It was one of the reasons he liked the guy and found him annoying at the same time.

Hiring Grant and subsequently making him partner had been Patrick's idea. Part of his "strategic plan," the man had said. All the more reason for Grant to make sure the business continued to gain ground in the spirits market. This meant staying loose, staying focused—and keeping his brain away from Stacey, at least while he was at work.

He frowned. That almost sounded like he was blaming her, or labeling her a distraction, but really, it wasn't her fault he couldn't keep his head on straight. Being with her last night, with that awesome dinner and the more than awesome sex after, made him feel... He didn't know what word to give it besides Patrick's "happy," as lame as it sounded.

Why wasn't he panicking about how she made him feel? Where was the well of fear that edged up higher and higher, the voice of caution that practically screamed at him whenever he was too close to having one foot into a serious relationship?

"Whatever it is that's going on in your personal life," Patrick began, "just remember that you're our spokesperson. Do your job, schmooze people, and don't taint our reputation." He frowned. "Oh, and keep making the best bourbon around."

"Do my job. Best bourbon. Schmooze. Don't mess up rep. Got it."

Something about his tone and the hard look he shot him made Grant's skin prickle. The guy was serious, but Patrick had a job to do, considering how much money he'd borrowed to open the distillery in the first place.

Patrick headed for the door that separated the distillery from the tasting room. "I'm off to give Stephan a break before he ends up mauled by the bachelorette party."

Grant blew out a breath. Stephan was the third partner who worked with the marketing team and handled the tasting room. Thanks to his playboy lifestyle, Stephan refused to mix business with any place he might run into an ex-girlfriend. That's when Grant was tapped to represent the distillery, thus earning him a piece of the company.

So it was time to get his head out of his ass before he gave his partners a reason to bail on him. He'd had enough of that in his life. No need to tempt fate.

Was he tempting fate with Stacey, though? Even in the absence of his usual fears, he couldn't shake the feeling that maybe he was, and he knew better than *anyone* how stupid that made him. No. He needed to pull his head out of his ass before he fucked everything up. As much as he hated the idea, one way or another they'd have to bring things back to normal. More nights in her bed weren't worth the loss of their friendship, were they?

He knew the answer to that. Had known it from the start.

How in the hell had he let himself forget?

He shoved a hand through his hair and remembered too late that he'd worn gloves. Though why he even had them on was beyond him, now that he thought about it. He was pulling ingredients for the mash, for God's sake.

Shit. He really *was* distracted. At this rate he'd start thinking he was making another batch of gin even though the juniper berries weren't in yet.

His phone buzzed in his back pocket. He grabbed it, his chest giving a funny little twist at the possibility of chatting with Stacey, and glanced at the screen.

Meredith.

Meredith? Who the hell was Meredith? He hadn't handed his phone over to a woman for her number since... Hell, he couldn't remember the last time. He scanned the text message. Oh, right. The woman Isaac had introduced him to at the Winters' get-together. She was available to meet for dinner tonight, then had a tight travel schedule after.

He frowned. Tonight was Tuesday. Therapy Tuesday. Table 13B would be set as it always was for them, and Mei-Ling would put them through the paces again, reminding them of all the reasons they were practically already a married couple.

Even as his heart warmed at the idea, he knew going down that path was a mistake.

He needed to do something to save him and Stacey from themselves, and fast.

He looked at the text message again. Maybe this was the universe's way of handing him an opportunity that would fix everything.

He blew out a breath, knowing what he had to do. It was as much for Stacey's good as his. At least, that's what he told himself. After all, he'd encouraged her to keep looking for Mr. Long Term despite what was happening between them. By going on a date with Meredith, even if he wasn't interested in the woman, even if the idea made him feel queasy, he'd prove to Stacey that he meant it. If a best friend couldn't keep his word, who could?

He thumbed a quick text to her, asking if they could skip this week's dinner, and almost immediately got a response back.

*Why?*

He hesitated, but if he was going to preserve their friendship, he had to do it, right?

*Meredith's got time tonight before she heads out tomorrow morning. Won't be back for three weeks. If you're not okay with it, say the word.*

And even though it made him the biggest idiot, his heart whispered, *Please say the word...*

Ten seconds later came the one-word response: *Fine.*

He frowned and texted back: *Are you sure? I don't have to go.*

He couldn't help it—masochist that he was, even knowing he could never do anything with it, Grant was desperate to hear Stacey tell him she didn't want him to go. If she couldn't—if this was headed the way every other relationship he'd ever been in had gone, he wanted to know before what felt suspiciously like love turned into a nightmare that ripped his heart out of his chest.

*Please tell me not to go...*

Stupid heart.

When she didn't respond right away, he set his phone down and headed to the storage area for a sack of barley to start the whiskey. His hands shook as he reached for the bag. Why was he shaking, damn it? He needed to get a grip. No matter what she said, he had to get the batch blended before he left for the day.

After he'd hauled the sack into the room and dropped it on the floor far less carefully than he should have, he picked up his cell.

*Go. Have a great time! Catch up with you later. XOXO*

A strange, achy sensation struck him dead center in his chest.

There it was.

And he wasn't surprised.

# Chapter Seventeen

Stacey sucked in a deep breath as the hospital elevator gradually came to a complete stop. She could do this. Julian and Martha depended on her. They'd hired her to create a good experience, a memorable experience. A *fun* experience. Julian's orders.

She would put her own heart, still crushed after Grant stomped all over it, aside.

There would be no tears, no sadness, nothing to remind them that they were having their last dinner together in a hospital room instead of in their backyard like he'd hoped.

She clutched the insulated picnic basket in one hand and adjusted the strap of a shopping bag over her shoulder. The elevator doors slid open and she stepped past two nurses in hospital scrubs, talking animatedly in a foreign language.

How Julian had managed to convince hospital administrators to let her cater a meal was beyond Stacey, but she'd have fought for it herself if the older man hadn't been successful. Fortunately, he'd been an influential member of the Milestone community for decades. No doubt hospital administration was eager to accommodate one of their best patrons.

Walking down the brightly lit hallway, she glanced at the door numbers, and did her best to keep her mood as elevated as she possibly could. *Julian's orders.* Martha had enough to deal with as it was.

"You must be Stacey," a man said when she passed the nurses' station.

"I am." She retraced her steps. "I think I'm headed the right way?"

"You are." The nurse indicated a hallway off to the left. "Julian's waiting. He's very excited about having you here."

"How's he doing?"

"Hanging in there."

Probably code for "no improvement."

"Not great, huh?" Not that she expected the guy to divulge anything.

The nurse gathered up some paperwork and straightened them. "He's a fighter. With the privacy laws, that's all I can say," he added. But the sad smile on his face told Stacey all she needed to know.

She bit down on her lower lip. She was on the brink of wanting to know, and *not* wanting to know. Curiosity won. She eased in a deep breath, then slowly blew it out. "How much longer?"

The nurse hesitated, scrubbed a hand over his neatly trimmed beard, then nodded as if making an executive decision. "A day, maybe two. Hard to say exactly, but it'll be soon."

*Oh, God.*

Stacey nodded. She needed to get a grip. On top of losing Grant, this was going to be tough, but she had to do it. Julian and Martha depended on her.

"Thanks for taking good care of them."

He flashed an easygoing grin. "Thank *you*. Julian's talked nonstop about how much joy you've brought him and Martha, about how much the two of them have been able to recreate some of their fondest memories because of you. Not too many people have that kind of outlook when they're… faced with these circumstances. But you've been instrumental in making it a little bit easier on them."

"I never thought of it that way." She'd started Dinners for Two for hapless guys who couldn't cook and still wanted to impress a date, but she'd come to understand it was for so much more than that. "I guess I'd better go set up."

She walked the long hallway, concentrating on the preparations she'd have to make, and mentally cataloging the ingredients she'd brought with her. Foie gras and french bread. Pumpkin soup with crème fraîche. Goat cheese for the beet salad. Some good olive oil and aged balsamic vinegar that Julian had raved about in the past. Lavender shortbread cookies and a carafe of decaf coffee.

Thank God Carly could squeeze in the time to throw this last-minute meal together.

Yes, she'd brought them all. Including the vase with the single red rose that Julian wanted to give Martha. Just like the red rose he'd given her on their first date all those decades ago.

She stopped just outside his room. Okay, it was time to get her game face on. With a bright smile, she entered the old man's room. "Hey there."

"Hello, love," Julian whispered. He held out a hand to her. "I'm glad you're here."

He looked so fragile, cradled among pillows, with an IV line connected to a point on his arm and an oxygen line placed underneath his nose. Yet through it all, he smiled as if there was nothing unusual about where they were or why they were there. "Did you bring the foie gras? Martha loves foie gras."

"I did." She dropped her bags and set the rose on the corner table, then walked the short distance to his bed. She clasped his cold hand between her own, and an odd sense of peace surrounded her, a feeling that she was helping and not helpless. "She's gonna love it." Stacey looked around the room for a place to set up.

"I've asked for a table to be brought in," he said. "Should be here any minute. Now," he squeezed her hand, "tell me, what's going on with you and your young man. Quickly. Before Martha gets back."

And just like that the mood was shattered. Reality intruded, and along with it was the realization that time was nothing but an illusion. An illusion born of necessity, but an illusion nonetheless.

"Julian, don't worry about me." She smiled. "I'm going to be fine."

His shrewd eyes latched onto hers. "Are you?"

"Well, sure. I mean, it's not like Grant and I won't ever be friends again." A sharp stab struck her chest, and she quickly glanced away. *Were* they even friends now?

"You're no longer friends?" His voice was gentle, caring, the way it always was. How could he be even remotely concerned with her relationship with Grant under the circumstances?

Julian smiled weakly, and as if he could read her mind, he said, "We know what's going to happen to me. Right now, I'm more concerned about what's going to happen to *you*. You've a whole lifetime to walk through, and a lot of experiences waiting for you. One of the experiences I don't want for you, young lady, is regret."

Would there be regret if she broke things off with Grant for good? To not be friends anymore? No more Therapy Tuesday. No more Netflix. No more hikes or bike rides or kayaking down the river. Could she really do it?

"So tell me," Julian said, grasping her hand. "What happened?"

She swallowed back the pain. She'd cried her eyes out at Carly's that night, and she was pretty sure there were no tears left to be shed. "He canceled our standing date at The Chinese Stop so he could take another woman out instead."

The pain intensified, catching her off guard. Maybe there were still tears holed up in there, not that she'd let them fall. Sharing what had happened was one thing—falling apart was another. "I'm sorry, Julian." She attempted a smile and tried to pull herself together. "It seems silly to care so much about stuff like that."

He nodded sympathetically. "I'd hardly call it silly." He shifted. "Is it possible you were mistaken about the other woman?"

"No." She clasped her hands together. "He made it pretty clear, and he's well within his rights to go on a date. I mean, we're best friends and all, have been since we were kids, but he doesn't owe me anything." Nothing like loyalty or...love.

The old man chuckled.

"What?"

"When you're my age, my dear, it amuses me to hear you say that you're anything *but* a kid now." He coughed. "But, please go on."

She shouldn't share so much, but something in his kind tone and smile tugged the words out of her. "Well it's just that I was beginning to think he was someone I could have more with. But it turns out he's just like the others."

And, really, it served her right for indulging in thoughts of a possible happily-ever-after with him. Despite her feelings, reality told her something completely different. Reality told her she needed to take Grant Phillips at face value. He didn't want a relationship—he'd even told her to keep an eye out for her Mr. Right—and she'd been dumb enough to think he'd change his mind. She should know better. Not even burning an offering at Chinaman Hat would overcome Grant's resolve.

"The others?"

Julian's question pulled her back to the moment, something Grant would've teased her about. Grant again? Ugh. She needed to get him off her mind. "The other guys I've dated. There's always something wrong with them. I mean, they start out great and stuff, and then one day I realize that something's not quite right with the guy."

She frowned. "Take the last guy, for instance. Turned out he was a cheating jerk." And she was more than happy to be rid of Leo.

"Good reason to walk away from him, then, but I'm sure you've dated others."

Clearly Julian wasn't going to drop it. She rested a hip against the hospital bed. "One guy had a thing about gluten. Wouldn't touch a piece of bread or get within three feet of one."

"Oh, he wouldn't eat a piece of bread." Julian nodded sagely, the corners of his mouth inching up. "I can see why you broke up with him."

"Are you making fun of me?" Julian's smile was so contagious, she couldn't help but mirror it.

"Of course not. Now, go on."

"Well, another guy insisted he do all the driving whenever we went anywhere. Like he didn't trust my driving at all."

"Which meant that he'd have to cart you everywhere. *Tsk, tsk*... What was he thinking?"

"You *are* making fun of me."

"Maybe a little." He smiled. "I hope you're listening to what you're saying, my dear. Aside from the cheater, were those true reasons to reject a potential suitor? Or maybe someone else was the reason?"

"I don't know." She shook her head. "It's like none of them were right. Like they weren't *good* enough."

"Yet Grant is good enough?"

She shrugged. "Sort of. Except he's not interested in anything serious with me." Which was the suckiest part of the whole thing. The dull ache started again, drawing her in so that she had to fight hard to keep from tromping down that path.

The old man sighed with a smile and shifted on the bed.

"Do you want some help?" She straightened. "Should I get someone for you?"

"No." He waved her off. "I'm fine. Just trying to get comfortable. But back to you and Grant."

"There is no me and Grant. Falling for him would be extremely stupid. All I wanted was for the two of us to be willing to explore where this relationship might go."

God. She sounded whiny and pathetic. How the hell had she been reduced to this?

"Is it possible," he began, ignoring her comment, "that you were involving yourself with men you subconsciously knew you'd never commit to because it was always about Grant?"

Stacey blinked and tried to get the words to make sense to her.

"Well, no…" Stacey felt the heat sear her face. Aside from Leo, was it possible that's why every man she'd ever dated was lacking somehow? Because she didn't really want a serious relationship with any of them? She glanced at Julian, saw the wisdom and the kindness in his eyes. "Maybe?"

"You are the only one who can answer that, my dear. But know this: love is the greatest gift that can ever be given and received. It is worth having, it is worth finding, it is worth waiting for."

"Julian's right, you know."

Stacey turned at the sound of Martha's voice behind her. "You make it sound perfect."

She carefully walked into the room, each stride assisted by her leopard-print colored cane. "Oh, goodness, no relationship is perfect. Look at us. We've had our rough spots, but what relationship doesn't? When you find love, and if you're brave enough to reach out and embrace it, that love will transform you, making you better than who you were. But finding that kind of love means finding a heart that hears yours."

The words were so beautiful, so romantic, they strummed a chord deep inside Stacey. This was what love was about: a gift that inspires a person to be the best version of themselves possible. She wanted that so badly she felt the intensity down to her core.

"What if he doesn't?" She hesitated, not sure how much to say. "What if he doesn't recognize my heart? Then what?"

"I promise, if he's the one, he will." Martha's smile radiated from her even as her gaze locked onto her husband. "And, like Julian said, I also promise it's worth finding."

She huffed out a breath and frowned. Grant *had* tried to text her that night, wanting to see her, but she'd replied that she needed space, needed a break. Thankfully, in true Grant fashion, he'd respected her wishes and hadn't made any attempts to reach her since.

That was two days ago. Two long, miserable days.

Martha stepped around to the opposite side of the bed, and Julian's gaze followed her. "How are you feeling?" she asked, taking the hand her husband offered her and squeezing it gently.

"Like we should break out of this joint and go salsa dancing," he said softly.

Martha grinned. "I bet I can distract that hunky nurse

while Stacey busts you out of here. We'll meet up in the parking lot."

Based on what she'd witnessed, they were right. Love was a truly powerful force, bringing out the best in a couple even through life's crappy times. Love was definitely worth fighting for, but it was up to both people in the relationship to make it happen. Clearly, Grant wasn't fighting for the relationship. She stifled the sudden burst of pain in her chest and forced herself to face facts once and for all. Grant wasn't "the one."

Now she just had to figure out a way to move on with her life.

# Chapter Eighteen

Grant maneuvered his truck off the highway and toward the two-lane road to the boat ramp. It was a perfect day to take the kayaks out. He just wished Stacey were with him.

But no. He'd tried to do the right thing and *still* managed to fuck everything up.

The whole thing was a mess, but what the hell was he supposed to do about it? She'd asked for space. How was he supposed to make things right when he couldn't even talk to her?

Damn it. He *knew* this would happen.

He backed the truck onto the boat ramp, cut the engine, got out, and slammed the door. A glance at the truck bed showed that the kayaks had made it in one piece, even if his brain hadn't.

The passenger door slammed. "Are you finally going to tell me what's wrong?" Aidan asked when he reached his side. "Or are we playing twenty questions like we did back when we were kids?"

Grant hauled himself over the tailgate and onto the truck

bed. "Nothing's wrong," he told his brother. He quickly undid a strap and stepped over one end of a kayak, then made his way toward the back of the cab.

"Like hell it isn't." Aidan climbed onto the back with him. "I'm barely off the plane last night when you text me, insisting we go kayaking today. You even played the birthday card. When have you ever done that? I mean, I know I was out of the country on your birthday and everything, but you sure as hell didn't expect me to cut my honeymoon short for it, did you?"

"Don't be an ass. Of course I didn't." He straightened and propped his hands on his hips. "If you're gonna be back here, at least grab the paddles and put them together or something."

"You're changing the subject," his brother said, reaching for the paddle sections. "And for someone who insisted we hit the lake today, you're not being very sociable."

Grant jumped off the bed of his truck, then pulled one of the kayaks over the closed tailgate and onto the ground. "Sorry. You're right. How's married life?"

"Honestly," Aidan said, snapping a paddle together, "I have to admit, it's pretty great." He had a shit-eating grin on his face.

"Yeah, well, you're lucky you found her."

"No argument there."

His brother might've found someone to share the rest of his life with, but Grant had been shown time and time again, in no uncertain terms, that finding someone special—*being* special to someone—wasn't in the cards for him, despite how badly he wanted it to be.

There. He'd admitted it.

Not that wanting what he'd never have changed anything.

Grant made a beeline for the cab of his truck to grab the life vests he'd thrown in the back seat. He pulled the vests out and stopped. Shit. He'd brought the vest normally reserved for Stacey.

"What's wrong with you?" Aidan asked after he returned.

"What do you mean?"

"You're too quiet."

"So? Can't I just want to lay eyes on my big brother?"

"Sure." Aidan raised an eyebrow. "Only, you've never done that before."

"Fine. How was Puerto Vallarta?"

Aidan set the paddle down and stared at him. "You don't give a fuck about my honeymoon, so why don't you tell me why we're really here?"

Grant hesitated. Did he really want to go through the whole Stacey thing with his brother? He reached out a hand and gripped the top of the tailgate. "I don't understand women," he finally blurted out.

"Join the club."

"I mean, one minute she's your best friend and then the next she throws you away like a lifetime of friendship doesn't matter anymore, just because you screwed up. It's flipping complicated, and I—"

"Whoa. Wait. Are we talking about Stacey?" His brother eyed him. "Because the last time we talked it was Lucy or something like that."

"That was a long time ago." He blew out a breath and scanned the lake behind them. Had it been that long since he'd talked with Aidan? Damn it.

Aidan let out a low whistle. "So we *are* talking about Stacey."

"Yeah. Only, she's not talking to me now, and I'm pretty sure we're not going to be friends anymore after this all pans out."

The ache he'd managed to keep at bay since he'd gotten her text message asking to be left alone swept forward in full force. He sucked in a deep breath to assuage it, but to no avail. This was fucking worse than screwing up a batch of bourbon worth several thousand dollars, no matter what Patrick said.

"Well, it's about damned time." His brother slapped him across the back. "I wondered if you'd ever come to your senses."

He glared. "What do you mean?"

"You two are good together, right? You've been pretty much inseparable forever."

"Haven't you been listening? It's not like that anymore."

"Okay, tell me what happened."

"We got together. It didn't work out. Now she wants me to leave her alone." And there was that sense of dejection again, like a heavy blanket glued onto his shoulders that he couldn't shake off no matter how hard he tried.

"Is that the CliffNotes version?"

Grant folded his arms.

"You're going to have to fill in the details sometime."

"What more is there to say? I tried to avoid making things worse. She walked away."

"That's still not telling me much. What do you mean you tried to 'avoid making things worse'?"

Grant blew out a long breath. He might as well come clean. "I canceled Therapy Tuesday so I could take another woman out to dinner. I was afraid we were getting too close and needed to make sure we weren't about to ruin our friendship."

He slumped against the side of his truck. "It was a dick move—I get that now—but really, I just wanted her to tell me not to do it. Like maybe knowing she was in just as deep would make everything okay. Instead, she told me to go. Like me taking another woman out was perfectly fine. And then when I texted her later to tell her how I felt, she asked me to leave her alone because she needed space."

Aidan crossed his arms. "I'm waiting for the part where she was somehow at fault here."

Grant threw his hands in the air. "She *walked away*, Aidan. I may have the world's shittiest luck when it comes to this, but I really thought we were strong enough to get through anything."

"I suspect there's more to this than you're saying, but let's stick to the salient points. Basically, you believed her when she told you to go ahead."

"Yes."

Aidan rolled his eyes. "What the fuck was she supposed to do? Stop you when it sounded like you wanted to go? What self-respecting woman would do that? She'd have taken it to mean *you* didn't want *her*. And rightfully so."

"But I didn't go through with it," Grant said. "It took less than five minutes in the lobby of the restaurant to realize I didn't want to be there. I left before our table was ready, but when I got to The Chinese Stop, Stacey wasn't there. Mei-Ling said she never showed up."

"Go on."

"I headed to her apartment, fully intending to get us back on track, but her car wasn't in her parking spot. That's when I texted her and she told me to leave her alone."

He'd read that text at least a hundred times. When he first saw her words, fear worse than any pain he'd experienced before tore through him, stronger even than when he realized his mother wasn't coming back.

That same fear raked over him now.

Aidan leaned a hip against the tailgate. "Considering all the effort you went through to keep your standing date with Stacey, I can't believe she'd tell you to leave her alone. I mean, what a way to make a woman feel special."

"Very funny, wiseass." His shoulders slumped. "She made this incredible dinner for me a few nights ago."

"She made you dinner. Care to elaborate?"

"It was more than dinner."

"I don't need to hear the details."

Grant frowned at him. "I was going to say, she'd found some things I remembered from my childhood, things I'd lost along the way. The toy car...the map of Alaska...even the funky kayak candleholder... She found them on eBay and a bunch of thrift stores and then she created this dinner for me."

"That *is* her business, you know."

"And she's damn good at it. She made the evening really special, Aidan. Like it was the most important thing in the world for her. Like *I* was important." And that's how she'd always treated him, wasn't it? Like he mattered, like who he was and wanted to be *mattered*.

Then he had to go and fuck it up.

Grant scrubbed a hand over his face. "Shit."

"So are you just going to give up?"

"It's no good. She doesn't want anything to do with me, with us." And that was the hardest part to accept. To not be able to see her, call her, touch base with her regularly... It didn't matter if it was for serious stuff or stupid stuff, either. She'd always been a short distance away, literally and figuratively, and he'd loved that. He'd have done anything for her, and God knew she was always there for him.

*Was* now being the operative word.

Aidan shook his head. "You give up too easily."

"No—"

His brother waved off Grant's protest. "Look, do you want her in your life as a friend or as someone more? Someone you can come home to at the end of a long day, someone you can laugh with, dream with, someone you can share life with?"

Grant stared at his feet. "It doesn't matter what I want."

"Like hell it doesn't." Aidan shoved his hands in

the pockets of his jeans. "You have to decide if this is a relationship worth having, and if it is, you have to figure out what you need to do to get her back."

That was all well and good, but... "I'm scared." He squeezed his hands by his sides as the words shuddered out of him. "What if it doesn't work out? What if she leaves, too?"

"I know," his brother said quietly. "But in your mind, she already has left. I don't agree with you, by the way—asking for time to think isn't walking away. Either way, what's the worst that can happen? The way I figure it, you still have to try. Assuming, of course, that you want a real relationship. Relationships aren't perfect all the time, you know."

Grant cast his brother a sideways glance. "You think you're revealing some huge secret?"

He shook his head. "Let me finish. They're a give-and-take kind of thing. There's negotiating that takes place, even if that isn't a particularly sexy way of putting it, but it's true. And most importantly, there aren't any guarantees. You and I both know that."

Considering their pasts, yeah, Grant was well aware of that.

"You have to step up anyway," Aidan insisted. "You have to fight for what you want, for what's important to you." He shrugged. "Or you can give up."

Grant stared at his brother. "Let me guess. Giving up isn't an option, is it?"

"Sure it is. But is it one you want to take? I mean, is it the way you want to live? Let me ask you this." He pulled the tailgate down and sat on it.

Oh, great. Aidan was in classic thought-changing mode and there was no way to stop him. Grant braced himself.

"What if you'd given up after you went into the foster care system? What if you ran away or gave your foster parents hell? Where would you be now? Owner of a distillery, or possibly in jail or worse?"

His brother had a way of not mincing words.

"What if I had? Trying to do the right thing never made a difference. I was still shipped off to someone else every couple of months."

"Would you be half the man you are now if everything had gone differently?" Aidan challenged. "Would you have the same resilience? The determination to succeed? You say you only want to live in the now, but I've never seen someone hang onto their past as hard as you do. Why? Worse, why keep hanging onto the habits that don't make your life better?" He cocked his head. "You still have the letter, don't you?"

The quietly spoken question seemed to carry on a breeze off the lake. Grant hesitated, then nodded. "I do."

"And you read it on your birthday."

"I have it memorized," he admitted.

"That was a part of your past. So, tell me, what's been the best part of your life now?"

"Stacey." Her name was out before he had a chance to get his filters in place. He turned his attention back to the kayaks. "Is being married to Delaney turning you into an armchair psychologist or something?"

Aidan laughed. "No, but she makes me think. It's one of the things I love about her." His voice turned serious. "With the right person, your life becomes far more than you'd ever believe possible. I promise. The question you need to ask yourself is if you think Stacey's that person for you. And if you think she even *might* be, then go after her. And not as friends with benefits, or whatever you had going on."

"And if I fail?"

"Failure isn't a bad thing. It just shows you that a particular approach isn't one that's going to work. Then you try something else after that."

"Are you suggesting I stalk her until she caves? That's

creepy."

"Moron." Aidan glared. "I'm suggesting you make another effort to win her back. And if the answer's truly no, then at least you can move on knowing you did everything you could. Next time, you won't trade a good thing because you're too scared."

Grant straightened. "Are you calling me a chicken?"

"I'm calling you a dickwad who's going to have to undo the mess he's made of things with the woman he obviously cares very deeply about."

"How the hell am I supposed to do that?" His shoulders sagged. "I totally fucked up."

"Look. You had a tough past. No one expects you to be perfect, least of all Stacey. She's been with you from the start, and my guess is, she'd be more than willing to be with you again. You just have to figure out in your own head what you want with her."

What he did know was that life without Stacey in it on some level was unimaginable. But was he capable of going the distance with her? He wanted to, but that didn't mean anything.

He stared out at the lake, at the calm water and the way the midday light shimmered off parts of it. That was what Stacey was to him, wasn't it? She shined her light on him and brought out the best parts of who he was. "I love her."

It was true. He loved her. Deeply. Which was why he couldn't bear the thought of not having her around.

"Did you tell her that?"

Grant blinked. "Sorry, I didn't realize I'd said that out loud." He shook his head. He was seriously losing it.

"Well, did you?"

"No, I didn't."

He told her he was going out with another woman instead.

Aidan should just kick his ass and get it over with.

"What are you waiting for?"

"I can't waltz into her apartment and blurt that out." Could he?

"You're the only one who can know that."

Aidan stood in silence across from him while Grant processed all the ways a declaration like that could go wrong—and *right*. Gradually, the noises from the lake registered. Kids laughing as they splashed close to the shoreline. The droning motor from a passing boat. Birds screeching as they flew overhead.

Grant looked past his brother to the deep-blue background behind him, to the point where the water kissed the sky. This place…it invited laughter, cultivated friendships, made memories. And that's when the idea took hold.

"Maybe I can't just waltz into her apartment, but maybe I can show her instead." He pulled out his phone and tapped on the screen. "I'm going to do what she did. Sort of."

"Atta boy…I think."

It didn't matter what his brother thought; it didn't matter what anyone thought. Grant knew what he had to do. It might not work, but Aidan was right. He had to try harder.

He only hoped it'd be good enough.

# Chapter Nineteen

*Home again, home again.*

Stacey climbed the stairs to her apartment and sighed. Too bad there wasn't anything more exciting waiting for her on a Friday night than dinner and Netflix. Which was pretty much all she could handle. Between her business clients and lack of sleep, she was exhausted.

She stuck her key into the lock and pushed the door open, then stopped as several things registered all at once.

The lights were on.

Sounds were coming from the kitchen.

Music was playing.

Something clattered onto the counter. "Goddamn it."

Her heartbeat kicked up at the sound of the familiar male voice. "Grant?" She shut the door and nearly tripped on her way toward the kitchen. "What the—?"

She stepped carefully around the trail of wooden spoons…measuring cups…a kitchen scale…a couple of spatulas…and something that looked like a paintbrush. She blinked. Were those envelopes scattered along the trail?

"You're here," Grant said, a goofy smile on his face.

"What are you—" She looked past him, and only then did she notice the condition of her kitchen. Every pot and pan she owned was out. Every lid right along with it. Cabinet doors were opened, and half the contents of a drawer were on the stovetop. "—doing?"

"I thought I'd make you dinner."

He looked half excited, half apologetic as he followed the route her gaze had taken. And he looked so damned cute with her apron tied around his waist.

"Is that what this is supposed to be?" She propped her hands on her hips and looked around the small space again. "Cleanup's going to be a bitch."

She tried to concentrate on that thought, but couldn't. Instead her gaze darted back to Grant. He was here. Now. And damn if her heart couldn't stop registering that fact. If she wasn't careful, it'd beat right out of her chest.

But she couldn't stop the warmth that spread through her, couldn't stop the way her pulse picked up speed, either. Grant was here. Even after she'd sent him away, even after she'd made it clear that she didn't want to see him again, he was here. That had to mean something, right?

"Ummm...I kinda think I might've gotten in over my head."

"You think?" She pointed past him at a bubbling mess of something on the stove. "What's that supposed to be?"

"Risotto. I tried to get ahold of Carly for some advice, but she's not answering my texts."

"She's pissed at you."

"Oh." He shrugged, obviously undaunted. "I decided to go it alone. Thanks to Google." He held up his phone, that goofy grin back on his face again.

She read through the recipe. "You know you're supposed to stir it on low heat, right?"

"Yeah, about that. I wasn't sure what low was, so I started at the bottom and worked my way up when it wasn't cooking fast enough."

"Why?"

"Because it wasn't cooking fast enough. I wanted it to be ready when you got home. I thought I just told you that."

"Really?"

There was no way to stop the small smile on her face. He'd done all this, gone through all this trouble. For her.

She looked around at the mess. "I'm not sure if I should laugh or cry."

"Look, Stacey, I'm sorry. I promise I'll clean it all up." He reached behind his back and pulled off the frilly apron, a gift from Carly that was supposed to inspire Stacey to do more than heat food in the microwave. "Can we please just talk? Since, obviously, having dinner ready for you isn't happening here."

"This should be good." She leaned against a free spot on the counter and folded her arms. "Go ahead. Talk."

"I screwed up."

"That's not news."

He nodded. "I screwed up royally."

"Try for something *really* new, Grant."

He blew out a breath and looked at the floor. "This isn't going to be easy for me to admit, but when I asked about canceling Therapy Tuesday, I wanted you to tell me not to go."

She frowned. "You mean you were testing me?"

"I guess you could call it that." He frowned, concern washing over his face. "I wanted you to tell me not to go, to tell me that you were looking forward to seeing me, to being with me."

"Do you have any idea how much that hurt me?" she asked quietly. "Knowing that you wanted to go out with another woman? After everything we'd shared together?"

"I *didn't* want to go out with her. And I didn't go through with it, even when I thought you wanted me to." He shook his head. "It took me a while, but I finally figured it out."

"Figured what out? That you didn't want to go out with her after all?"

"No, what I *want*."

His face had that edge of vulnerability to it, one she'd seen several times when they were kids but thought he'd outgrown.

"I was too scared of the idea of us, of this," he continued, pointing between the two of them. "I was so sure that I'd lose our friendship if we got too close, so sure you'd walk away. I didn't want to risk it."

She frowned. "First of all, we've been pretty close since we were eight. Did you honestly think anything would change that, especially if there was an 'us'?"

His shoulders slumped. "All I know is that my mother walked out on me. If she could do it, anyone could. So it didn't surprise me when I was shuffled from foster family to foster family. It's like I wasn't worth having around, you know? But right from the beginning you were always there for me. You made it all bearable." He shook his head. "Just the thought of losing you, Stace… I couldn't stand it."

"You matter to me, Grant. You always have. At the heart of it, we both want to know that we matter to each other, right?"

She stepped toward him and reached out a hand, and when he took it, a zing of electricity pulsed through her. Would it always be this way between them? God, she hoped so.

"You'll always matter to me," he said quietly.

She looked around her kitchen. "I can see that."

"I'm so sorry about Therapy Tuesday." He blew out a breath and glanced up at the ceiling before lowering his gaze to capture hers. "Please believe me when I say that hurting you is something I never want to do again. Ever."

His eyes told her everything she needed to know. In their depths were trust and hope and vulnerability. "I believe you."

Was now the right time to tell him? To pour her heart and soul out for him to see? She looked away. Really, she had nothing to lose, and everything to gain.

"Grant?"

"Yeah?" He squeezed her hand, infusing warmth through her whole body and sending a trail of want chasing after it.

Stacey took a deep breath and kept her gaze on his. "I want you to know that I not only love you, but I believe in you, in us. And I believe that, no matter what, we're stronger together than we could ever be apart from each other."

He stared at her, and she saw the moment her words registered. "You love me? As in an action flick or rom-com kind of way? Because you should probably know I'm not romance material."

She grinned. "So then what's with the trail of kitchen stuff? I almost tripped on the spoons by the doorway."

"I thought that maybe we could spend some time learning how to cook together. You know, take a class or something." He scoffed. "Much better than *rose petals*."

"You actually shopped for kitchen stuff? Some of those look like the specialty kinds that Carly has, so I'm pretty sure you didn't get it around here."

He pulled out his phone and grinned. "Amazon. Two-day shipping."

"So you planned all this?" She felt her eyes go wide. "Mr. Live-in-the-Moment put a plan together? I'm impressed." She stared at the odd assortment that comprised the trail. "But what about the envelopes?"

"They're gift cards. You know, in case we mess up dinner and have to get takeout."

He planned this for her. The dinner, such as it was, the

cooking gadgets, the gift cards. Her heart swelled, threatening to burst with happiness.

She threw her arms around his neck and laughed. "Oh my God. Grant."

"Was that funny?"

"No." She pulled away and stared into his eyes, her heart squeezing at the sheer rightness of this man, this moment. "This means so much to me. I love it. And I love you."

He smiled and smoothed his hand over her hair. "Are you sure?"

"I'm sure."

He grinned. "That's convenient." Then his smile faded, replaced by a fierce intensity. "Because I love you, too."

"You do?"

"Mmm-hmm."

She looked back at the trail of gadgets and envelopes and pulled away. "Wait," she said, stooping to pick a well-worn envelope off the carpet. "This is the letter from your mom."

He nodded. "That's right."

"I don't get it. Why's this here?"

Grant gently took the envelope from her. "It's time I left the past where it belongs, and walk into the future I want. With you."

Before she could stop him, he tore the envelope in half.

She gasped. "Grant, are you sure?"

"Absolutely." He smiled, continuing to tear the paper until all that remained was a pile of strips on the kitchen counter.

Stacey blinked. "I think that's one of the bravest, most romantic things I've ever seen." She stood on tiptoe and quickly kissed his lips. "You want to hear something fun? Aside from Leo, who was a real douche, I realized that every relationship I'd ever had didn't work out because, deep down, I've compared every single one of the guys to you. You're the bar I've used, Grant, and it's obvious to me that no one's going to get close."

He brought his mouth down to hers and the kiss was so soft, so tender, so sweet. How did she miss seeing Grant all these years? How did she miss the strength of his arms or the way he touched her heart, touched her soul?

When he pulled back, the raw vulnerability in his eyes was more than enough to convince Stacey this was exactly where she needed to be. "I want you in my life, Stace. Not just as my best friend, but as something more, something deeper."

"I could go for that."

"That's good." He seemed almost relieved.

"Why?"

"Because I was prepared to do whatever it took to get you back into my life."

"Including cook me dinner?" she teased.

"Especially that."

She peered around him. "I think we need to use one of the gift cards."

"Pizza? I'll go get it," he offered.

"Oh, no, you don't." She tugged him close again and snuggled into his embrace. "I'm not hungry right now."

"That's too bad."

He caressed her cheek, his touch so light, so tender, she was sure her heart would overflow with love for this man. "How come?"

He pulled back far enough to stare into her eyes. "Because I'm *starving*." He held her face between his palms. "I've missed you so much, baby doll."

Then he lowered his head and captured her mouth in a sweet kiss full of promises made, and promises yet to be made. Of dinner and Netflix nights, of kayaking and bike rides, of Therapy Tuesdays at The Chinese Stop.

Julian and Martha were right. Love was worth finding. And in this moment, Stacey knew it had been worth the wait.

# Epilogue

*One year later...*

Chinaman Hat loomed in the distance, tall and imposing as always.

"Here's to Therapy Tuesday." Grant held up his teacup. "And to many more to come."

She grinned. "Goofball."

"You say that now, but I promise you won't be saying that later."

"Oooh, promises, promises."

"You can count on it." Passion laced his words as tightly as he squeezed her hand before releasing it.

Butterflies danced in her stomach, and her heart skipped. "I am."

True to Grant's word, they hadn't missed another date night at The Chinese Stop in the year since they'd been together, yet it still amazed Stacey how much things had changed in that time. He'd moved in with her a few months ago, her business had taken off, and now, with a silent investor, it looked like the distillery had another scheduled expansion in the works.

Across the table was her best friend. Pride washed over her with that knowledge. He worked hard, but also knew when it was time to pull back and relax. He was everything she'd ever wanted, everything she'd ever dreamed of.

And he was hers.

That fact swept through her, feeding the gratitude that continued to strengthen their bond.

She finished the last bite of egg roll off her plate. "About Saturday, Delaney texted and said to bring the kayaks to the baby shower."

"That's weird. Why?"

"She wants you to take Aidan off her hands for the afternoon. He's hovering and won't let her do anything, and it's driving her nuts."

"I get that. She looks like she's about to pop."

"Women have been giving birth forever, Grant. She's going to be fine." She tilted her head. "You wouldn't be the hovering type, would you?" she asked lightly.

He stopped, stared, and carefully wiped his hands on a napkin. "I don't know. Are you trying to tell me something?"

"God, no." She shook her head. "That's for some time down the road." She leaned against the booth and groaned.

"You doing okay?"

"I think I ate too much," she said. "I'd forgotten how addictive the egg rolls can be."

He laughed. "You always say that."

"And I always mean it."

"Here your fortune cookie," Mei-Ling said, plopping a small pot in front of her.

She studied the strange sight. "What the heck?"

Fortune cookies with thin strips of red ribbon hung like ornaments from a small tree. Stacey blinked, then looked across the table. "Grant? What are you up to?"

"Go ahead," he said, grinning. "Open one."

She slipped a cookie off a branch, then cracked it open.

She straightened the tiny piece of paper. "Please say yes." She frowned and turned the strip of paper over. "There's nothing on the back. What am I supposed to say yes to?" She looked around for Mei-Ling. "That doesn't make sense. Chef Dennis must've been distracted when he wrote this one."

"Actually, it does make sense." Grant slipped out of the booth and was at her side. He then dropped onto one knee.

"Wha—?"

He opened the tiny black velvet box in his hand and held it out to her. In the fading afternoon light, the single solitaire diamond in it sparkled. She blinked, pretty sure she was imagining things.

"Stacey Nicole Winters, I love you with every ounce of strength I have in me. Please be my partner, my best friend, my lover, my everything. Please say yes."

Mei-Ling passed by their table. "Yeah, you say yes now. I bring you more tea."

"Ma!" her son called from the kitchen. "Stop it. You leave them alone."

Stacey's gaze never left Grant's. "I'm guessing if I don't say yes there'll be a whole lot of explaining I'll have to do, huh?"

He swallowed, and the vulnerability in his eyes reached out to her, offering her all that she'd wanted, all that she'd hoped for.

"Only say yes if you want to, Stace." The words were quiet, humbling. That Grant could feel so unsure about her, about *them*, yet was willing to take the risk anyway, was the greatest gift he could ever give her.

Stacey grinned, and a delicious warmth spread through her. "Grant Adam Phillips...yes."

# Acknowledgments

I am so grateful to the many talented people who made this book possible!

Heather Howland, thank you for sushi and hand-holding, for believing in me, and always pushing me to be a better writer. I am so blessed to have you as my editor!

Meredith Clark, I'm so lucky fate threw us together! Your insight and structural knowledge of craft is amazing, and there's so much I've yet to learn from you. Thank you for not rolling your eyes (that I could tell, anyway!) and for talking me off the ledge. Every. Single. Time.

Tawna Fenske and Marie Harte, thank you for long talks, long walks, and lots of wine! That you seasoned authors share so much with a fledgling like me makes my heart smile.

My awesome fan group, Melia's Marvels, thanks for sticking with me on this crazy publishing journey. Here's to another book birthday!

Lounge Ladies, thank you for your friendship, laughter, and unconditional love, even when I'm pretty sure you'd like to sometimes shake some sense into me. You all ROCK!

Rhonda Pollero, thank you so much for the Facebook friendship, and for providing the movie suggestion that kicks off Grant and Stacey's first love scene. You rock!

And, as always, my heartfelt gratitude to the team at Entangled Publishing. Your hard work and dedication to authors makes me so proud to call Entangled "home."

# About the Author

A native of Guam, Melia Alexander is the author of sassy, sexy, fun contemporary romances. She's fortunate to work at The Male Observation Lab (a.k.a. her day job at a construction company), where she's able to observe guys in their natural habitat. She likes to read, catalogue her shoe and handbag collection, and search out the perfect sunset, preferably with a glass of cabernet sauvignon and a box of dark chocolates. In an attempt to balance out her life, she also attempts to conquer her CrossFit fears: ring dips, power cleans, and the dreaded 800-meter run. Stay in touch with Melia on Facebook, Instagram, and her newsletter.

*Discover the* **Driven to Love** *series…*

DRIVEN TO TEMPTATION


*Also by Melia Alexander*

MERGER OF THE HEART

***Find love in unexpected places with these satisfying Lovestruck reads…***

## JUST ONE SPARK
### a novel by Jenna Bayley-Burke

Firefighter Mason has searched his whole life for a woman who stirs his soul. When he finds her, she's nose-deep in a racy paperback atop a vibrating washer. He's rushed into fiery situations before, and this woman is totally worth the risk. He'll just have to prove to Hannah that first impressions can be wrong and their spark of attraction is oh so right.

## THE BEST MAN'S PROPOSAL
### a *South Beach* novel by Wynter Daniels

Left dateless in a flamingo-pink monstrosity of a bridesmaid dress, Niki Hamilton decides to drown her sorrows in a glass of tall, dark, and handsome. When firefighter Grant Powers's best friend's new sister-in-law falls into his arms, he enjoys the experience a little too much. Then a rental snafu leaves Niki temporarily homeless. So, gentleman and masochist that he is, Grant offers his spare bedroom. Now, they just have to survive living together for a few weeks…

## TEN DAYS WITH THE HIGHLANDER
### a *Love Abroad* novel by Hayson Manning

There's no way Callum MacGregor is going to let a gorgeous American turn his hotel in the Scottish Highlands over to bored tourists looking to satisfy their *Outlander* fantasies. But if he can get go-getter Georgia Paxton to slow down and see the magic of the town and its people, maybe he won't have to run her out of the county…or his heart.

Made in the USA
San Bernardino, CA
26 March 2018